MONSTRODDITIES

Edited by Ben Walker

Web: sliceduppress.com / bluesky: sliceduppress.bsy.social

Cover art by Hannah Comstock – hannahcomstock.com

Table of Contents

A NEW AND DIFFERENT HUNGER

Tiffany Morris

There were so many ways to scream. Blood-curdling: deep, immense, primal, rumbling up from the gut. Yelping: fear swallowing itself and spitting back up. A screech: like an eagle, like its prey. A cry: surprise, tears, startled softness.

All of those screams were coming from the field.

A cabin: a mile from the beach. Sighing shoreline. Tall grasses. Plenty of tree cover. If you'd taken a helicopter over it, you'd have seen a jagged, snakelike coast, water coiling and biting at the rocks. The coast eroded and evaporated. Displaced creatures kept moving inland. The homes hadn't moved—they were safe for the moment.

That's where she'd first found them. A mile from the beach, her own backyard. A field of silhouettes in the fog. Silhouettes that she knew: graceful, unworldly, powerful.

Horses.

She hadn't wanted to approach; too much risk of spooking them. She knew that from her childhood, from the summer she'd spent on Aunt Jo's farm.

She stood, silent, still.

Yes, she knew horses, Aunt Jo had owned five of them: appaloosa, fallabella, breeds with exotic-sounding names. Aunt Jo's living room was filled with horse-racing trophies and ribbons, gold galloping figurines. It was a world shinier than the bottom of a beer can.

Erin had loved being on that farm, even though it sweltered in the heat and everything stank. It was staggeringly alive: there were wildflowers and bees and hissing barn cats, mean and fat on the bodies of field mice. At night, the barking of coyotes filled the sky.

"They've made their kill," Aunt Jo would say, a smile spread across her face.

Erin spent her days with Aunt Jo, tending to the horses, marvelling at how her tiny aunt handled the rough work of the farm. Aunt Jo was like no-one Erin had ever seen: ropey muscle and scraggly brown hair flecked with grey. Sunken eyes. Her face was unworldly and beautiful, betraying her unknown origins: Aunt Jo had just turned up beside the river behind the family's farm, something red and bloodied in the water, her clothes tattered and teeth chattering.

"The poor thing couldn't even speak," her mother had said. "We took her in and let the police know, but no-one had ever reported her missing. So, you know, she just became one of us. Things were different then, of course. She would've ended up in the system if it happened now."

Erin knew, of course, that that wasn't the whole story; that Aunt Jo had no memory of where she'd come from, had been prone to night terrors and sleepwalking and disappearing into the inkdark river where the family had found her. She would leave wet and muddied bare footprints from the front step up to her room, scowling as she scrubbed them down when she awakened. Erin, too, was a sleepwalker, though she never seemed to leave the house; she'd wake suddenly, most often at the back door, with no memory of dream or how she had gotten there. The family kept five locks on the door, just in case, armed only before the house went dark with sleep.

After that summer on the farm, leaves sighed and stretched their golden haze over the world and Erin mournfully returned to the city, to school, to a world of homework and bullies and bus routes. Her mother had returned one night from Aunt Jo's, her voice full of tears and face drawn. Erin sat outside the locked bedroom door and waited for a signal, listened for a return to calm. Her mother's sobs were interspersed with the croaked snippets of a phone conversation: *unidentified, entrails, disappeared.* Erin had known what *presumed drowned* meant. The river had finally taken Jo back.

When they'd gone to the farm to pack up her stuff, most of the traces of Jo had already vanished. Erin went into the barn. The cats had fled. The horses were long gone, the stable silent without them. She peered into one of the stalls. The hay was trampled with hoof prints and matted with pools of dried blood. When she walked down to the river, the sun was slung low on the horizon, and the metallic tang of death writhed in the steady, trickling water.

When Erin stood in that field outside her cabin, the night full of billowing fog and those graceful grazing silhouettes, she wasn't at all surprised to hear Aunt Jo's voice.

"Look at them," Aunt Jo crooned. "Look at those lovely horses."

* * *

Erin hoped the horses would come back in the daylight, where she could be easily seen. She carried a sandwich bag filled with corn kernels, apple slices, anything to coax the horses to her.

There were no farms for miles. How had they gotten there?

She walked along the field, crows circling overhead. She walked through the field and through the trees until she hit the empty shore, where the grey waves broke hard against the large, jagged boulders.

Infinity hummed and sang in the rhythmic crash. Erin sat and chewed on an apple slice, savoring the tart sweetness. The beach stayed empty the whole time she was there, grey on slate on stone. The humid summer air was silver and stinging. She thought again of Aunt Jo, and how similar they'd been: adoptees with somnambulism, odd folks with an intense draw to the water. Missing her aunt was a sharp ache in her side: who knew what kind of person she might have become if she'd grown up with Jo's company, her influence and empathy. Erin was glad that, like her aunt, she got to live away from the city and its strangling architectures, its alien world of machine noise and crammed bodies; away from those places where she'd never felt she fit.

She left the desolate beach, savoring the dull sunlight as it beat down upon her face.

* * *

Erin drank the last of her glass of wine and placed her dishes in the sink, gazing out the window. Spring peepers sang their chorus. With nightfall, the horses might have returned.

She grabbed the bag of apples and corn from the fridge and enjoyed its coolness against her skin. Taking the flashlight from the counter, she slid the screen door open and walked out into the dark yard. She made her way to the field, where silhouettes bowed and neighed in the deepening haze of night. The spring peepers started and stopped in unison with each step she took. The silence was a breeze breaking through the dark.

Her heart leapt as she moved closer to the horses. The silhouettes stopped and turned to her. The smell of blood carried thick in the humid air. Her stomach clenched. Were they injured?

One silhouette was lying on its side. Erin shone her flashlight over to it. A deep redblack pool soaked into the bleached grass. She moved the light up. The beam was clinical and bright against the wet intestines spilling from the carcass, its splayed-open abdomen.

Erin screamed and stumbled backward. Her hand reached out and hit the side of a horse, its fur sticky and matted with blood. Her hand rolled over its emaciated frame, the jutting bones poking out from under its skin.

This wasn't right.

Horses mourned their dead.

She turned around and stepped back again, shining her light on the horse she'd stumbled into. Its massive black eyes gleamed lantern-bright in the flashlight. It snorted, impassive, its face drenched in blood.

The horses were devouring the carcass.

Erin dropped the bag. Her screaming chased her back into the house.

* * *

Dim daylight crept between the fingers of the cabin window blinds. Erin had slept a fitful sleep, cut through with images of carcasses flayed open, writhing maggot rot.

She fumbled through breakfast, unsure of whether she should check the field in daytime. What if they were still there? The yolk of her eggs were smeared across her plate. The greasy smell filled her nostrils and her stomach jumped into her throat in revulsion. She was ravenous and nauseated all at once. A waste: she scraped the remnants into the garbage and did the dishes, squinting out the window. She couldn't see the horses.

Erin put on her boots and, with unsteady feet, made her way to the field.

It was empty. No birds sang there. All was stillness and stifling silence. Sweat beaded on her lower back. The grass faintly trampled, faintly stained, smelled sweet and rotten.

With nightfall the horses might come again. In the field, in the dark, they'd lie in wait.

* * *

Five nights passed, and she hadn't dared go into the field. Erin conjured the images of the horses in her mind readily; each time, fear transformed into guilt. Their food sources must have been dwindling if they'd resorted to cannibalism. Their jutting bones writhed and shifted in her memories.

Maybe they just needed different food. She could give them some of her supply. Erin ate a last forkful of rare steak. She savored the blood on her tongue before swallowing. Horses didn't usually eat meat, but maybe they'd developed a

6

taste for it. Her own hunger had grown insatiable; her stomach a snare snapped open and begging for prey. She'd stocked up, filling her grocery cart with foam package after foam package screaming bright red in the fluorescent supermarket light.

There was plenty to go around.

Night fell and she went back to the field. Raw, bloody hamburger seeped through the plastic wrap of the package and onto her hands. She resisted the urge to take a small handful and let it dissolve on her tongue. The sodden Styrofoam tray left a trail from the house to the field.

The skeletal silhouettes were already there.

"Hi," Erin said, her voice shaky. She reached out a tentative hand to pat one of the horses. Its thin frame was a word spoken into wind.

She took a wet clump of meat from the package and held it out to the horse.

A clamor of neighing came from the creatures. They did not take the meat. Erin set down the package and stood, helpless. What did they want?

She caught her reflection in the horse's void-black eye. Aunt Jo's face smiled back at her.

These creatures had a new and different hunger.

One of the horses began walking in the direction of the water. Its eyes glowed red when caught in her flashlight. She knew she had to follow it, to see where it had come from. As she took unsteady steps behind it, the other horses stayed still and disappeared into shadow. Erin kept the bluewhite beam of the light trained in front of her as she followed the horse to the shore.

The water grew louder. Under it, the faint sound of screaming erupted staccato from some distant field. It eventually gurgled into silence. Then there was only water once again.

A sliver of waning moon glinted softly on the crashing waves. The horse ran from her sight: a pounding sound as it dissolved into the ocean. Panic ran through Erin's legs as she froze in place, fruitlessly moving the beam over the shoreline, looking for the strange creature.

A surging roar thundered around her as a herd of horses emerged from the ocean, hissing and screeching, running forward in shadows and moonlight, lines of scales glinting beneath their tufts of fur. Erin dropped her flashlight and screamed, her legs finally propelling her into motion. Her feet stumbled over rock and sand as her seaweed hair bounced and danced in the wind. Her spine bent and shifted in agony as her bones thickened. She fell to her knees and found herself not stopped but running, her new black eyes watching the foam break against rock as her kelpie skin absorbed the light.

She could taste the blood waiting for her. She ran into the field, staggeringly alive with want. Her new form was a memory of home and hunger. It was a promise of devouring.

IN ALL OTHER RESPECTS RESEMBLES A BULL

Sarah Peploe

They were going to walk home. Granted, there would be a sea in the way later on. "But we'll cross that bridge when we come to it," Tomas said, and he chuckled and nudged Alger. Tomas was all chuckles and nudges, questions and chatter, observations: the heat and what it had done to their rations, the cold and what it was doing to their scars. His friendliness was insistent, almost aggressive. It was as if his blather was a rope thrown down and they were both climbing up it, hand over hand, pulling themselves back into the world.

As if the world would take them after the things they had done.

Even if they did make it home, Alger knew there would be questions. Maybe accusations of desertion and cowardice—and the desertion part would not be a lie, but if any man called Alger a coward, Alger would knock him dead. He supposed this was another bridge that would be crossed when they came to it. He nodded at Tomas now and then, he offered some mindless little bit of speech like "You said it, brother." Another hand up the rope. They kept walking.

It was a well-trodden road they were on, to the coast. Tomas and Alger had removed their colours, but the people they passed still looked at them crooked. The ones who held bundles and babies clutched them closer. The last of those had been two days ago. Now the road was only settled dust and the odd bone. As day cooled into evening, Tomas and Alger veered from the path and through the forest in search of food. They drank silty water from a stream with no fish, and took turns watching through the night with Alger's crossbow, waiting for beasts to come and slake their thirst. None did.

In the morning they chewed bark and started walking again, parallel to the road. It was chilly, still. There was a mean milky sun like a little hole jabbed in the sky. The trees thinned out before them. They could have borne left and re-joined the coast road, but over to the right, beyond the last few trees, there was a great field.

Tomas and Alger hesitated. They had learnt to be wary at the edges of places. The field looked tended, with rich soil in furrows. Further off there was a figure, lumpen and indistinct in the dawn like the rounded haystacks the men had torched, months back and miles away. It moved. It came closer.

It was some kind of bull, and sat astride it was a child of indeterminate sex, one of the horrible ugly little scraps that passed for children here, with their bodies too young and their faces too old. They made Alger pine for his own lovely children. This child was filthy, with rat's-fur hair. It wore a too-large, much-mended tunic and a knapsack with a spade strapped across the top, sticking out either side of its shoulders like a milkmaid's yoke. Everything dwarfed the brat, and it was already small. The bull was huge, the child almost doing the splits across its back. It was shaggy-necked as a lion and all over the same sort of colour, brown-orange-black like a smoky night. Horns thicker than Alger's arm.

There was no-one else to be seen. Alger looked to Tomas and Tomas to Alger. Tomas could speak without speaking, when he had to.

They stepped out of the woods together as the creature passed their hiding place.

"Good morning," Tomas said.

The—*girl?* Alger thought—barely nodded. The bull paid them more heed, turning its wet pebble eyes down towards them, blinking slow and not quite with both lids at the same time. A thread of spit twinkled from its mouth. Alger noticed its horns were wrong. They curved inwards. The tips were pointed at its own head.

The girl wiped her nose on her wrist and scratched her bare leg. She had little marks dappled up her calves. They looked raw and sore. Alger hoped it wasn't catching. But there were white scars there too behind the fresh lesions, so it likely wasn't something you could die of.

"That's some beast," Tomas went on, smiling and puffing out his cheeks. "What are you feeding him?"

"What he finds. Same as any of us," she said.

"Mm," Alger said. He didn't raise the crossbow yet, nothing so obvious. Just readied his hands on it. They'd need it for the bull, but the child wasn't worth a bolt. That bull. Weeks of meat. Roasted first. After that they could dry some in the sun, to last them till they reached the coast. It could even last them all the way home. At home, Alger would go amongst other people and he would not loathe them for not having seen what he had seen, he would love the bones of his wife and children and never speak to them of any of it. But he could tell them he had seen a bull the size of a cruck house, that part he could tell them.

Something flared in the girl's eyes, too sullen to be alarm, too callused to be fear.

"Mister," she said.

Alger snorted. It was to be expected, this fawning, he'd heard it before, how they'd wheedle for sweets one minute then curse with ferocity and inventiveness past their years the next. She entangled her fingers in the bull's mane.

"He's all we have," she whined.

"Then you're rich indeed," Tomas said. "Richer than us."

At that, Alger lifted the crossbow. The girl's expression didn't change, though she must, Alger thought, be well aware of what such a weapon could do, a child like her, a child of this land. Behind her, Alger could see the bull's tail, comically uplifted like a dog's.

The bull stepped back. One hoof scraped the earth. Alger snorted again and said "Girl, if your glorified bullock charges us he'll drive his horns into his own brain, such as it is."

"He won't," the girl said.

And sudden as a thief she bounced on the bull's back, jabbing its ribs with her rag-wrapped heels. Its hooves quivered in the soil—then it started to turn away, giving its back to the soldiers. It was so big, even its escape attempt was laborious, like a galleon in retreat. *Too slow*, Alger thought, *too late*. He could pierce its neck easy from here, send it to its knees and the girl head over heels over its thick skull, the earth doing half their work for them. He took aim.

The bull shat. No cowpat, but a great spigot-spray of green-black liquid manure, gouting from its hind parts. It doused Alger head to hips.

In less straitened circumstances Tomas might have laughed. Now he turned, one hand poised to scrape the filth from his friend's eyes, the other to grab the crossbow, for the bull was lolloping away now—but Alger was staggering back, spinning like a dervish. Tomas saw that there was not steam but *smoke* rising from him, not the cosy warmth of a cowshed but real, evil hell-heat, and with it a nightmarish and throat-clenching stink, midden and meat, cooking flesh.

Alger was shrieking and flailing. Tomas whipped off his jacket. He had put out a fire in this way once before—an honest fire, with flames you could see, and it hadn't done the burnt man much good in the long run, but still. . .

He reached for Alger, to wrap the garment about him. Alger's finger clenched blindly on the trigger of his crossbow. The bolt slipped neatly through Tomas's throat.

The girl kept her heels down. Teaching a bonnacon not to flee too far was the thing. It was their nature to run away, shitting lavishly as they went. It had served them well. She clung to his mane and edged her way up till she was almost sitting on his neck. From there she could scratch his ears and shush him. He slowed down, bellowing still, but more as a man who has won a fight, letting a friend drag him away saying enough. His warm, kiln-smelling hair was like reins between her fingers. She coaxed him to a halt.

The girl lowered herself from his back, bending her knees as she landed. It was her mother who had taught her to do this. She had a memory of being small and fat and lying puppy-peaceful in the curls of the bonnacon, and a woman showing her. Knees like clean bowls and puffs of dust rising from her feet. Or maybe it was a thought. Usually the girl knew when she was lying, she was good at it, but about her mother she didn't know. She tried the memory on her aunties and Auntie Mups had said: *You never knew your ma, she went before you could piss in a pot.* Auntie Nith said: *Oh let her think it, what's the harm?*

The girl returned to where the men had fallen. The one who'd been shot was already dead, face-down in a great red pool undisturbed by bubble or pulse. The burnt one was still twitching and screaming, tiny little screams like a licked finger on glass. She finished him with the spade. Auntie Mups had taught her that. Then she delved in the knapsack for the penknife and the sack, and her uncle's old gauntlet gloves. They engulfed her, as Auntie Ren had said once, which made her think of gulping and throats. *And every time,* Auntie Ren had gone on, *you take them off, and your, you know, your little paw there, comes out, it's still a surprise that it's not his hand. Her Daddy's face, her uncle's gloves, her granddad's spade, she's a little motley of men, isn't she. A mixed bag,* and Auntie Nith had cursed fit for a man and left the room.

With her hands swallowed in leather, she set to slicing away the burnt one's ruined clothes. She wiped the corpse clean as she went. It might have looked like reverence, from a distance. She gathered the rags, and the skin that came off with the wiping, in the sack. The bonnacon came closer and laid down, tucking its legs underneath its great body, to watch her work.

The girl yelped with joy when she saw that the shot one was wearing leather boots. His feet were much bigger than hers, but she could stuff the ends. They would come up over her knees. Another part of a man to make her up. No more blisters from the splatter, though. No more picking and itching into orange sores. She knew she ought not to scratch them but it felt so good and no-one ever told her off for it.

Once the bodies were passably naked and clean and salvaged, she gave the bonnacon's neck a kiss to reassure it; this next bit always made it uneasy. She took the axe from her knapsack. Dung that burned everything it touched did not make for good fertilizer. But blood and bone did.

LAWS OF CONTRACTION

Joe Koch

Slinking into work late again under a hood of dead skin, Crawdaddy Creech creeps into his cubicle adjacent to Hoss. The ten gallon white hat lifts and tips in greeting. All Creech sees of Hoss is the signature hat and a white mountain through the semi-translucent Plexiglas divider until big man is ready for a break.

A dig between phone calls reminds Creech his tardiness hasn't escaped Hoss. "Greetings, partner. Glad you decided to drop in and join us today."

Creech wheezes in reply, unable to combine the right syllables to stand up to Hoss. Some kind of sound oozes out.

Whatever he says isn't right. He knows it by the fluid squeezing out of his skin. The foreign cloak is sensitive. Any wrong move sets it off. Creech tries to keep still underneath. His motto is: *keep calm and carry the dead weight.* He'll be trying to pay some bills or maybe nuke a burrito at night or engage in any common, honest act when the skin imposes its agenda. Going clammy, rigid, or fevered, it swathes him like ropey diapers. Creech can't move or talk too loud without his big dead skin getting upset.

Hoss keeps ragging him cheerfully. "Someone stayed up late with a special lady last night. Hoo, boy. I like those special ladies. Anyone I know?"

A blurred enigma through the divider, up and down waving motions like wings with the disappearance of the white hat suggest big man is fanning away feigned sympathetic lust. Creech should say something clever that supports chuckling assent, but he needs to clock in and the letters on his keyboard are gone. His dead skin weeps. Damp sweat sheathes his forehead and fingers. Dripping hands slick over the buttons and skid across the desk. Knuckles bang the plexi with an unintended punch.

Creech apologizes, immediately regrets it, hates himself for wanting to take it back, and apologizes again.

Hoss laughs and brays one of his favorite tag lines. "Tear it up!" He's been making the same embarrassing jokes since they were kids.

Their noisy exchange disrupts the office pall. Disapproval plucks at the wet folds of Creech's overused garment-like hooded skin. It's thick the way his daddy told him to grow it, yet somehow the excess surface area reverberates wildly after all these years clinging to Creech's dermal fat: it overreacts.

Creech freezes at the blank keyboard. Time keeps ticking by and Creech looks later and later on paper and he can't clock in. The skin constricts around his belly like a boa snake. He can't manage a deep breath. Coworkers eyes crawl up his back. Sensing them, the skin flushes and quivers. The hood closes. Drawstrings pull the circle closed around his face, closing Creech's eyes and muzzling his mouth.

Charged like a magnet by the old man's missives, Creech can't break the habit of catching all the loose skin that sloughs off around him and holding on to the dead parts everyone else drops. Inclined to help, he saved his family from their own filth. They thanked him with disgust. Creech worked harder and harder to please, amassing a generous layer, but the skin never calloused correctly. It's grown an independent life, needy, reactive, and wet.

People can practically smell it on him. It's the sort of smell people like to punch. Displaced anger inflames the other office workers' eyes, fingers, and feet. They glare, drum, and twitch, preparing to attack. The skin sags in submission.

Hoss tips his chair back, an elephant performing a tightrope act. Burly arms invade the personal dead end maze of each of the workers like lab mice seated beside him. Hoss clears his throat of a voluminous loogie. He swirls it around thoughtfully before he hawks it into the trash. Surveying over the plexi dividers, Hoss hunts the hostile room for challengers. An army of hateful eyes like timid mice retreat down the row of cubicles. The rodents bury their noses in their screens. The skin loosens and allows Creech to breathe.

Hoss glows white at Creech through the textured plexi blur. He laughs, and the plastic dividers rattle across the office in their metal frames. The modular rows of attached workstations shake. None dare look up to confront him.

Happy, Hoss takes a sales call. The thunder of his voice blasts food particles out of the crevices of Creech's keyboard. Stink bug carcasses cascade from undusted corners. Window ledges release cracked paint. The cubicle rodents cower harder and hunker down while Hoss spins in his chair and orates.

"How do you do, Mr. Smithson, sir. Well, if it isn't goddamn hot as a dog's balls down here, I don't know what. How's the weather treating you up there in Atlanta today?"

Seeing his chance to escape the next threat of attack, Creech makes a beeline to the men's room under the cover of Hoss's voice. He huddles inside a stall trying to get the skin calm but it billows and puffs up with worry because he still hasn't clocked in.

Hoss helped Creech get the job, always helps when Creech can't function. Creech owes Hoss a better effort than hiding in the john. The guilt stresses the sensitive skin more than ever and keeps Creech trapped in the stall.

Unable to see straight or breathe deep under the heavy cloak, he tugs at the elastic suit of flesh holding him hostage. Creech twists the earlobes into reddened knobs and tries to pull the hood off. He grips a slab of thigh meat like a sandbag hauled from a truck bed and tries to toss it off. No matter how far he throws it, his wretched mantle snaps back.

He shoves four fingers in each side of his mouth, clamps his thumbs against his fingertips vice-like through the soft skin of the cheeks, and peels open a hole to free his smothered skull.

The doughy mass swells to meet his grip and squeezes out through his fingers. Creech's pliant exposed smile mocks the broken teeth shattered by grinding rage encased within. He struggles as the hood billows over his hand to flap closed over his mouth again. Creech can only dream of stripping the whole thing off, lips and all; he chokes on the thought, cries with his pants down at his ankles as though the ruse in the stall required demonstrative proof.

"Ladies and gentlemen, that is what you call working the system and getting the job done. That is how we do business, my friends and compadres." Hoss harangues the whole office with his success. He's so loud from his cubicle Creech can hear him from down the hall all the way through the bathroom walls. "Now if you all will pardon me a moment, I've got some business of my own to attend to."

The cheap strip mall building's floor sags and whimpers under Hoss's strides. Creech feels him coming in the lilt of the linoleum and buckling of the flimsy hinges. The door and the floorboards squeak with escalating complaints, but no amount of protest can hold Hoss back from seeking relief.

Farting and harrumphing, Hoss fills up the stall adjoining Creech's temporary hideout. Odorous blasts and dangerous creaks blare in the interludes between Hoss's heaving sighs of contentment on the seat. Confident in his right to take up as much space as he can find, Hoss rocks in the stall while Creech's skin ripples into a knot wishing for a way out.

The whole room is full of Hoss, barricading the exit and exhausting the supply of air. Creech crouches as the man expands.

Pink fat from the next stall presses into keyholes and doorframes, filling every gap as Hoss bloats gregariously, happily. He's always been the extrovert. Creech recoils from the invasive pink paste though he's strangely attracted to its gel-like motion. He wants to touch it before it melts, but the skin objects, cinching tight, trussing his fragile finger bones into an impotent fist.

The stalls rock. The room shakes. The fat loses its form and floods the floor in a slippery pink pool. Creech lifts his feet. Warmth rises from the unctuous free-flowing fat. Excessive heat from Hoss's seat degrades the strict fibers of Creech's forbidding skin and undermines its caustic grip.

Creech's bones unwind with quiet need.

He plunges an emaciated finger into the glistening pink putrescence and pulls up a fine fleshy globule. The heavy hood he carries retracts into a writhing clump cowering behind his back. The skin that binds his hand drapes like a languid robe from the wrist, leaving Creech free to sink the savory stuff into his watering mouth.

New glands open in the slackened false skin. Pores like gestational sacs grow individual snails with meticulous claw-feet that tug free in search of shells. Muscles lurch away on hooked tines, crawling and swimming into Hoss's stall through the flood while Creech sucks the pink gunk off his finger, relieved of his proxy in mere seconds with shocking ease.

The dead skin runs down, livid and bloody, leaching excess liquid from Creech. It happens so fast, he doesn't have time to hold it back. Shuddering as if he's naked even though his core feels strangely warm, strangely certain and strong, he tip-toes out of his stall trying not to splash. Conscientious, he heads to the sink to wash his hands. Instead of the misshapen tumor he's used to, Creech sees a normal man standing in the fogged mirror.

He wipes away the veil of moisture with a shirtsleeve to make sure it's not a mirage. There he is, brown hair with a little bit of grey, grey eyes with a little bit of brown, not too old and not too young, and just a hint of office paunch. An average shaky figure in the unforgiving glare of fluorescent light, Creech shakes while his abandoned skin calls to him with the crushing litany of a drunken evangelist.

Hoss hollers. Creech kicks in the door of his stall. The door bounces back at Creech, who dodges it sideways, jumps into the stall, and stops. Weaponless and trapped, he gapes at the thing on the toilet.

A shivering mass rises. Pink strips like car wash flaps shimmy down from a white ten gallon hat. Sliced, sinewy smears of a skin-shroud glimpse around ripples of raw pink flesh. Snail-scummy and jagged with eyeholes badly-placed, the meat-ropes twist in convulsive roiling, unable to envelop the mounded fullness of Hoss's magnificent excess.

The towering wide assemblage holds out its hands, beckoning. Without a thought, Creech goes into the open arms.

Creech pushes through the meat-flaps and leans into the flab blanketing the big man's chest. The Hoss-thing holds him. The boundaries blur between bodies as the flayed cloak weeps with adhesive fluid. Creech clings to the human host beneath. Snail fingers scrape sensitive flesh and bring a sound out of Hoss that shakes the walls. The mirror shatters. The lightbulbs pop. The skin slips, puddles, and unspools with a liquid whisper.

The rejected skin slides derelict into the center of the sloped floor and disappears down the drain.

Creech is covered in rich juice. Hoss is slicked, a white and pink blur. A big blurred hand cups Creech's brittle shoulder. Creech braces for the sensation of snakes strangling his chest.

Nothing happens.

Rid of the suffocating caul, unrestricted air flows in and out of his lungs. Creech stumbles a little from the sensation of flight even though he's standing still. The white blur bolsters him, expressionless. Creech laughs out loud at the weightlessness: his shoulders, his backbone, his feet.

Movement feels like he's floating free on buoyant sea-foam, or like he's surfing the air on a magic carpet's lilt. He almost falls over, spinning toward the exit in a bold pirouette.

"Easy there, partner."

It should be Hoss's voice but it's not.

The impulse to apologize slows Creech's feet. He starts talking and balks at the volume. He stops spinning before the empty stalls. He's concerned with what he sees. The big man in the middle of the bathroom under the blown out lights blurs away into a milky blob.

Blurs out and vanishes like he never was there at all.

MY LOVE, MY LOVE, MY LOVE

Ai Jiang

Tongue slit down the middle
    like a snake, then tied in
    a ribbon atop a gift, present—
    Hair hanging drenched
    in blood and oils from weeks
    of unwash, dampened by light
    drizzle of rain and swamp mud.
    They were drawn to it,
    like flies to corpses, yet
    separate like oil and water,
    and frozen in place by it,
    like tongue on metal
    in the middle of winters.
    It whispered, "My love."
    And the man frozen
    by the edge of the swamp,
    murky water bubbles stopped
    in time by the frigid air, frosted,
    just as the man's feet
    were iced in place, immobile.
    "My love." The voice lingered
    in the man's mind. His heart
    chilled. It drew closer. His lover's
    features replaced its face—the one

the same colour as the swamp,
with its popping boils, rotten
weeds, dead barks entrenched.
It whispered, "My love."
The man screamed with his eyes,
his fear stopped, dissipated
at his fingertips, cold then
numbness drenched him in sweat.
It—his lover widened her lips,
snaked out was the tongue
like a ribbon, slit, caressing
his face and throat and—
It was human, it was human,
it was human, until it was not.
"My love, my love, my love."

THE SIN EATER'S WIFE

Avra Margariti

The clawfoot iron tub is etched with healing runes,
   the bathwater a tepid affair.
   My knees freeze against the winter wasteland
   of cracked bathroom tiles, dress soaked
   in the spillover, arms swirling
   aquatic shapes and signs I cannot yet speak
   into being.
   You are awake but not aware,
   held in saline water, smaller and weaker
   than I know your body and soul to be.
   The man whose hunchback I had to cut you out of—
   butcher knives and amputation saws—
   had tarry tobacco breath
   with which he called you a creature
   of sin, an abomination, a tumor
   far from benign.
   There's room for tenderness here
   but not for gentleness.
   The man's flesh and blood cling to you
   like lice or leeches.
   Fragrant soaps and lavish loofas
   pushed aside, I scour and scrub
   your battered body into cleanliness
   until once more I can see in you

my inamorata imp:
your webbed toes and fingers
like delicate lace,
your pomegranate seed tongue,
arachnid eyelashes and doe eyes
in perennial possession of innocence
no matter what your barbwire teeth devour.
How deluded all your hosts are
to name you the sin
when it is their rot you feed on.
You don't remember me yet but, soon, you will.
Call me Ananke. My stitches sting
as they sew your torn self back together.
My medicine burns in its necessity;
my needle, and my nettle.
I hope you can forgive this pain
once you're whole again—
but darling, you've always been most holy.

CABAL OF THE HOMUNCULI

Pedro Iniguez

Gazing past glass phials, and the flaming
    midnight oil,
    their countless small eyes roll sidelong,
    watching the Alchemist toil.
    He hurls curses
    at those miniature humans,
    their bodies submerged
    in gelatinous fluids.
    Though, unable to speak or slur,
    they mouth his every word.
    He tugs at his hair
    and they do the same.
    He sobs into his palms,
    and they imitate his pain.
    It is all they know how to do,
    as they try in vain to cater to
    their creator.
    He knows they are not his brood
    but his deliriums—skewed, chilling, insane—given life
    and agency in this mortal plane.
    They were borne of human seed
    fermented inside the wombs of beasts,
    their innards filled with solution
    of mandrake, brine,

and yeast.
They were to be his cherubs:
wholesome, loving, benign.
Yet, he is sure they are plotting,
speaking to one another through
language not yet divined.
Surely, they seek
revenge for their creation,
scheming, even now
in incarceration.
Yet, he cannot will to
see them killed.
Not by fire nor stabbing,
for the thought leaves him queasy and pale.
Instead, he will leave them marooned
in this existence, while he
drifts beyond the veil.
He pours boiling water into his cup,
steeping it with nightshade tea.
He sips the warm poison.
It trickles down his gullet and settles in his belly.
For a moment the homunculi observe
quietly. Then, their little limbs jerk like marionettes.
They thrash about wildly
like fish caught in a net.
Their tongues hang limply
out their maws,
mirroring the man on the other side,
their bodies now dormant in glass jars
beside their father for all time.

SONATA FOR RESTLESS SPIRITS

Lorenzo Crescentini
Translation by Amanda Blee

The Grand Piano for Demonic Induction was a bad idea right from the start. The clue was in its name, yet it was only when the dead rose up from the stalls of the Duse Theater in Bologna and poured out into the historic center that first the townsfolk, and then the national public began to realize the gravity of the aberration.

The idea for the instrument was relatively simple, brilliant, even: taking advantage of the same paths traveled for years by 'channelers' and widely explored by scholars and enthusiasts of the esoteric, the piano was tuned so that each key, when pressed, opened a channel which communicated exclusively with a particular spirit, whose tone of voice was noted in the score.

Unlike traditional instruments, the human voice is, by nature, malleable and fluid, capable of a range of two, three, even four octaves. However, when we scream or shout, whether in anguish, terror or pain, we always tend to reproduce the same note.

My agony is a D-sharp minor; yours could be a G or a B-flat.

With this simple consideration in mind, the wretched Bartimeus Ferraresi's Grand Piano for Demonic Induction was very similar, conceptually speaking, to any electronic keyboard.

There were two main differences, however.

The first was that tones corresponding to the various keys had not been sampled or auto-tuned, but researched and tuned with loving care, one by one: the Grand Piano for Demonic Induction was in effect a sepulchral choir of eighty-eight elements, each with its own imperfections. We scream our desperation in F perhaps, but if we prolong the note, we end up losing some of the frequency, wavering between E and D-sharp. It was precisely these imperfections, these faults, combined with the very specific timbre of the dead, that gave the *Sonata for Restless Spirits* its aura of decadent, desperate beauty.

There are no recordings of that accursed evening, but Maria Madàlena Ortega, rising star of Spanish opera and guest of honor, was one of the few survivors. In an exclusive interview, she described those voices as *the combination of a scream and a gust of wind in a forest of hanged men, who in life had never been happy.*

Ortega's words show her well-known dramatic vein. Perhaps someone else would have simply defined those voices as unpleasant, depressing, but the fact that she hanged herself only two days after she relived those memories leaves no doubt that the experience at the Duse Theater was, for her, deeply traumatic.

The second difference lies in the fact that the digital sounds of an electronic keyboard are known in every detail. They can be broken down into formulas and bit sequences, represented in graph form and modified mechanically at will, by twisting knobs and twiddling levers, or by virtual intervention on a specific interface.

By contrast, the sounds of the dead are summoned from an unknown land. Centuries of obscure rituals have taught us how to open doors that should remain locked, but no one can describe exactly what lies on the other side, in the darkness of the Beyond. In his wickedness, Ferraresi deliberately decided to ignore this particular aspect; danger and provocation were integral parts of his creations. Let's be honest; in the era of the shock factor, is it still possible to create art using only skill and talent?

Several years earlier, his controversial *Folksong for Flutes and Rifles* had been greeted with critical acclaim, while many more criticized the fact that the score expressly stated that the piece be played / shot towards the horizon, in a sparsely populated but not deserted area, and never, ever into the air. The low probability of hitting and killing a passer-by, with all the consequent legal and moral implications, was the very point of the piece, and therefore it could not exist without the threat of tragedy hanging over it. On the other hand, both sides agreed that the passage for the horn section was very pleasant.

Moving on from his *Folksong* to the *Sonata for Restless Spirits*, Ferraresi had made great advances in the musical aesthetics of death. Where the reckless composer learned the sacrilegious arts that lead to such progress is unknown, because he never revealed it, not even in his final interview (which, ironically, was published in the same magazine that included Maria Madàlena Ortega's last public words in this world).

During his interview/confession, Ferraresi took full responsibility for what happened that evening at the Duse

Theater and admitted that, if he hadn't gotten so carried away by his creative ecstasy in the long months of preparation leading up to the evening, he could perhaps have foreseen it:

The traditional channels of communication were sufficient to recall the voices of the dead, even obliging them to bend to the will of the instrument. But the agony of a lost soul is something remote, distant, at times almost subliminal. It is no coincidence that houses only creak at night, that ghosts drag their tired chains in the silence of huge, abandoned houses. All that separates our world from that of the dead is a veil, but this veil is the invisible equivalent of a heavy velvet curtain that absorbs sounds, obscuring them.

The last, and most demanding part of Ferraresi's work, it transpired, was in solving the volume problem.

The *Sonata* was composed to be heard in religious silence by small groups in a small, soundproof room, not in a packed auditorium.

Microphones were precluded: they would have distorted the tremendous purity of the song, confused those echoes of pure pain and erased the nuances. Not to mention that, according to the ethics of Ferraresi, who had absolutely no qualms about disturbing the sleep of the dead, any form of distortion between the voices of the dead and the ears of the living would have been an unforgivable insult:

There are millions, billions, of essences waiting over the threshold. Some of whom want to make contact. Others just want to be left in peace. But no one, I'm sure you agree, would be happy to communicate with the world they just left through speakers. The voice is all they have. For us, it would be like going back to our childhood home and hiding behind opaque glass.

So, in short, Ferraresi discovered how to resurrect the dead.

Resurgence, he called it. The only solution to the filter of the veil was to ensure the souls of the dead passed through the veil itself.

But he never dared to explain that, during his *Sonata*, the spirits would be forced to draw aside the veil that separates our world from theirs, recalled to an unbearable limbo, a pale imitation of life defined by the soundboard of the grand piano.

Perhaps the most fearless would have been attracted by the idea of a concert that violates the inviolable, but not the general public. Even the most alternative of the alternatives lives for the appreciation of those who pretend to scorn. More prosaically, two hundred sold tickets fill the belly twenty times more than ten.

(In this regard, please ignore the rumours that went around before the performance, which intimated that certain high notes harnessed the souls of Maria Callas, Freddie Mercury and other legends of modern music. It is highly likely that Ferraresi himself was behind those rumours, for publicity reasons. The high notes were nothing more than the voices of children who died violently.)

Ferraresi considered the procedure safe, as it was the pressure on the piano key that determined the connection with the place where souls were trapped and tortured at will, and its persistence. The moment the pressure ceased, that corridor between life and death collapsed.

However, Ferraresi had not considered the phenomenon he later called *spiritual interference* and which in esoteric literature is generally known as possession.

As soon as it was recalled, the spirit that dwelt in the G of the sixth octave flung itself at the pianist, the internationally renowned Hans Kovjac.

The audience watched helplessly as Hans' back suddenly contracted and his joints cracked hideously. The restless spirit would not allow Hans to leave the key, forcing him to open other passages. In what seemed like a carefully planned escape, Hans' fingers continued to press keys behind which the fiercest spirits lay in wait, thirsting for revenge. Where his fingers couldn't reach, his joints snapped and separated, forming unnatural chords of their own.

The audience began to scream when Hans' back turned in on itself and, in a rattle of broken vertebrae, his body came crashing down onto the keyboard. His legs followed suit, and soon after, eighty-eight voices intoned an atrocious cacophony.

Imagine how much resentment a soul condemned to centuries of darkness can accumulate, then imagine a chorus of eighty-eight of them, specifically selected for the agony conveyed in their eternal screams. Think what the audience must have perceived, what they saw and heard at the Duse Theater that night, as they surged outside, trampling each other. A boy and a woman were suffocated in the stampede and two old people died of heart attacks. The dead quickly possessed their corpses, slipping inside them, sending them out hunting.

Where their murderous hands failed to arrive, mass hysteria filled the void. Violence erupted wherever people believed they had cornered one of the risen, attacking before they were attacked.

Bodies fell then rose again, animated by a new, ancient life.

The dead fled the theater, tumbling into the streets of the old town.

Ferraresi was seen running away, crying. Whether his tears were the result of his *tête-à-tête* with the afterlife or of the failure of his greatest exhibition, your guess is as good as mine.

For a week after her escape, Maria Madàlena Ortega was harassed by the paparazzi. They tried to catch her out, to prove she was no longer the rising star of Spanish opera, but either an old pirate drowned at sea, a victim of the Holy Inquisition, or a soldier killed in World War II.

They did not succeed and, in the end, one of them invented the scoop that she was possessed by the spirit of an old gypsy woman, who had been murdered in a concentration camp.

Ms. Ortega released her famous interview and killed herself two days later.

Ferraresi managed to avoid arrest, fleeing the country and seeking refuge in Finland, where he lives today. After various telephone statements to the *Gaceta de Alagòn*, he refused to comment further.

When the police tried to enter the Duse, the agents in charge shot each other, and it was agreed that the passage created by the Grand Piano for Demonic Induction was not only still open, but had widened.

The area was evacuated, and a small, remote-control bomb was sent in, its detonation destroying the building. The first firefighter to approach the debris knelt down and gouged his eyes out.

Now the historic center is officially a red zone. No access allowed. An interdimensional black hole, an open door behind which the dead await their chance to grasp, return, rise again, be reborn.

The remarkable thing is, the Grand Piano for Demonic Induction was not destroyed in the explosion. It is still there, surrounded by rubble. No living person can touch it. And the thing that was once Hans Kovjac, and his long fingers, plays there every evening.

Those who live near the historic center of Bologna say that on windless days they can hear the dead sing. Their voices grow stronger, and theirs is a song of triumph.

THE DEVIL'S FOOTPRINTS

Tabatha Wood

Goddamn it, but it was cold working in the church. So cold that, if I stopped moving, I thought my blood and bones would freeze solid, and the Reverend would find my petrified body in the morning, hunkered like a gargoyle at his desk.

I peeled open a second cardboard box, the edges split and tattered. Like its predecessor, it was stuffed to the brim with old newspaper clippings, scribbled notes, and a mess of hand-drawn diagrams. All of it so-called research collected by the Reverend Eliot T. Harrow, vicar of the Parish Church of Saint Paul's of Dawlish village, Devon. All of it to be meticulously examined and catalogued as if it were crucial evidence in a murder case, not merely resources offered up to support a story.

I glanced across to the twin-bar electric heater humming away on the office floor. It glowed a vibrant orange, but the heat it threw out was minimal. I shivered inside my brushed cotton hoodie and pulled the cuffs down past my palms.

My editor had considered this little field trip to be an excellent opportunity. "It'll get you out of this stuffy office and into the open country," he'd said. Instead, I was 180 miles from London in the middle of a freak April snowstorm.

A slab of white built up on the window ledge of the vestry and crept against the panes. The snow had brought with it a blanket of silence as it settled and smothered the village. It felt later, darker than it should. I checked my watch to reassure myself I'd not somehow lost time and saw it was barely six o'clock.

I pulled the first piece of paper from the top of the pile. The words were written in neat but cramped cursive, black ink faded green with age. I chewed my silver pendant absentmindedly and began to read.

. . . a maximum of fourteen hours of darkness in which to make a forty-mile line of hoof-marks, all eight inches apart. At this pace, we can surmise the creature kept up an average of more than six steps per second from start to finish. Adding say, a further thirty percent for looping and turning, sees the creature taking ten steps per second over this continuous period.

This, I submit, is impossible . . .

I skimmed the piece for a name and date, finding it at the very bottom—*GM Robertson, naturalist, 1923*—and copied it into my notebook.

A sudden noise at the door made me jump, but it was only the Reverend Harrow. He bustled his way into the tiny office, brandishing two steaming mugs.

"Tea?"

"Oh, yes, please." I took the drink from him and tried not to grimace. It was milky pale and disappointingly weak.

"Sorry," he said. "There was only one tea bag left in the tin. I'll get Evelyn to get some more in the morning. Biscuit?"

He rummaged in his trouser pockets for a packet of custard creams, tore the plastic and held them towards me. This, at least, was a more pleasant offering. I took one and peeled it apart.

"My sister used to eat them like that," he said, as he watched me. "I never really understood why. You always end up with a plain boring bit of biscuit with no filling to enjoy." He spoke slower than the city voices I was used to, his vowels longer and relaxed, but his Devonshire twang was oddly soothing, and his tone put me at ease.

I used my bottom teeth to scrape the vanilla cream off the biscuit base and shrugged as I swallowed it whole. "Worth it, though."

"If you say so," he replied and nodded to the boxes. "How are you finding it?"

"A little tedious," I began, then saw his crestfallen face. "But, you know, it's all really interesting stuff that you've collected and I'm pretty sure it will make a fascinating story."

This assertion seemed to perk him up again. "I've kept everything I could find since the first sighting in eighteen fifty-five," he said excitedly. "All of Reverend Edgecombe's letters, and the reports that young John Worrall wrote. There are eyewitness accounts from the villagers living there at the time, and actual drawings that Freddie Campbell made when he was tracking the beast. All of it's in there."

"Do you believe it?" I asked, sipping tea.

"Well, yes," he replied, clearly surprised. "Don't you? Isn't that why you're here?"

I hugged the china cup with both hands to try to steal some of its warmth. "Of course I do," I lied. "I'm thrilled that I'll get to write this story. It's fascinated me ever since I was a child."

This, at least, was a partial truth.

The story of the Devil's Footprints had indeed fascinated me since I had first discovered it when I was nine in an old library book; an almanac of strange stories and amazing facts, including those of supernatural origin. The book had been withdrawn from rotation on the shelves and left out for quick sale. It had been the best 20 pence I'd ever spent, but I didn't believe a word of it.

The tale began that on the night of the 8th of February 1855, Britain was caught in the grip of the one of the coldest winters in living memory. Heavy snow fell across Devonshire in the southwest of England, including the village of Dawlish. When the villagers awoke the next morning, they found a trail of single-file cloven tracks, like that of a donkey's hoof, stretching for almost a hundred miles, from the River Exe to the River Dart.

It was said whatever creature made them had done impossible things. The tracks crossed roofs, went and over high walls, and disappeared through small holes in hedges. Sometimes they stopped dead on one side of a haystack, before commencing on the opposite side. Often,a trail led up to a house, as if *something* had stopped and peered into a window, or waited on a doorstep before disappearing into thin air. No one knew what had left them. The mystery remained to this day.

"Reverend Edgecombe told the parish it was the Devil himself, roaming the countryside in search of sinners. Not a bad way to entice people to join his congregation, I suppose," I laughed.

Reverend Harrow's cheeks went pale. "How much have you read?" he asked.

"Just select bits from the first box," I admitted.

The Reverend sighed. "So, you don't know the full story? Nothing about the missing people? Or the subsequent events?"

"I know the Dawlish footprints weren't the only ones. But they were the most impressive."

The Reverend drained his last dregs of tea and set the mug down on the desk. He stared at me for just a little too long, and I cleared my throat to fill the silence.

"Why are you here?" he asked, eventually.

"You called my editor and told them there was a story. He sent me and now here I am. What do you . . . ?"

The Reverend turned to face the electric heater; the orange light gave his cheeks a fiery glow.

"Freddie Campbell led a team of eighteen strong men to track the creature into Dawlish Wood: a pack of hounds and seven rifles between them. They cornered it, somewhere, deep amongst the trees, and the dogs came running back terrified. Campbell himself was a changed man, shrank from thirteen and a half stone to under eight in six months. Never again had a decent night's sleep. He said what he saw in the woods that day, he could never put into words, but it haunted him until his death, six hundred and sixty-six days after."

"Didn't Freddie Campbell die of diphtheria?" I asked.

"Ah, so you found the death notice."

I nodded.

The Reverend pulled a face. "That was the official cause of death, yes."

"But you think otherwise?"

"Do you know how many people disappear in Devon every year?" he asked, deftly avoiding my question.

"I'm sure I don't . . ."

"Almost two thousand. Most of them turn up, eventually; children wander off, young men get drunk and fall asleep in fields, etcetera. Many of the cases are unsurprising and inconsequential. Except there are a number whose disappearance is much stranger, who are sadly never found. Almost always during the winter months, particularly when it snows."

My eyes flickered towards the icy windowpanes. I hardly thought it could be possible, but the temperature in the office had dropped even lower. I hugged myself and set my jaw to stop my teeth from chattering.

"I tried telling the police when I figured it out. I showed them all the evidence I'd collected. They humoured me, as an upstanding man of the cloth, but they didn't believe." The Reverend swung around to face me, his dark eyes wild and wide. "He comes for them. I know he does. Those who are no longer devout. I pray for them all, as often as I can, but my flock grows smaller every month."

"Who comes for them?" I asked, feeling unexpectedly nervous, and my breath plumed like dragon smoke in the air.

"Isn't it obvious? The Devil," The Reverend replied, and despite the seriousness in his face, I couldn't help but snigger. The Reverend was not similarly amused.

"I told your editor to send me a believer. Someone who knew the risks! Did he not discuss this with you?" His eyes settled on the tiny silver cross I wore on a chain around my neck. I tucked it self-consciously beneath my top.

"What risks?" I asked, and skirted around the edge of the desk, putting more space between he and I.

The Reverend snatched a page of newspaper from the desk and began to read aloud. "The most puzzling feature of the curious hoof marks was not their alarming ubiquity, but their appearance in many strange and hitherto unlikely places. Tracks were found walking across a garden guarded by a fourteen-foot wall. They appeared on either side of dense hedges, haystacks, and even narrow drainpipes. Prints were seen on a bedroom windowsill standing two stories high. The creature, whatever it might have been, approached the doorsteps of several houses, only to then retreat."

He tossed the paper back onto the pile. "What do you make of that?"

"Well, I . . ." I began, but the Reverend had no interest in waiting for my answer. He snatched another clipping and continued to orate.

"At least twenty-three known cases bear comparison with the Great Devon Mystery. It does not seem unreasonable to suggest that there may be hundreds, perhaps even thousands, more cases that have been lost, covered up or simply never reported."

He glared at me over the top of the sheet. "That was written in nineteen seventy-two. I know of an additional forty-two cases between eighteen fifty-five and now. Do you know what else happens when the footprints come?"

I could feel the cold biting at my skin, nibbling me through my clothes. My knuckles felt tender and painful to touch. I could barely bend my fingers. From what he had already told me, it wasn't hard to guess what might be the answer to his question.

"People go missing?"

"People go missing," he repeated. "People like twelve-year-old Rebecca Harrow. Disappeared from her bed one snowy night in nineteen seventy-six."

I swallowed the lump that had lodged in my throat. Hoped what I was about to ask was wrong. "Your . . . sister?"

The Reverend nodded. "Do you believe in the Devil?" he asked me.

"I'm Church of England," I replied, by way of explanation.

"Do you believe in the Devil?!" the Reverend roared, and slammed both his fists on the desk.

"I believe in the Father, the Son and the Holy Spirit and that Christ died and rose again!" I spluttered.

The Reverend stood up straight and smoothed his shirt. "That doesn't answer my question."

Stacked snow covered most of the windowpanes now, and the sliver of sky beyond the pale had turned an inky black. I trembled involuntarily, from both chill and trepidation. My forgotten beverage, once piping hot, now sported an icy sheen.

"I was sent here to cover a story," I said, my voice sounding small and unsure. "That's what my paper does. We report on strange phenomena, unusual sightings, and supernatural events. We're not the first to cover the footprints, but my editor thought enough time had passed, there might be some interest in them again."

The Reverend refused to look at me. He seemed engrossed in a damp patch on the floor. "I worked it all out, the pattern. From dates and times and eyewitness accounts. I knew where he'd get to next. But every time, I'd miss him, see? I was always just a little too late. When this position opened up four years ago, I knew it was just a matter of time."

A rattle at the window startled me, a shrill scrape across the glass. Tree branches, perhaps, blown by the wind. Except the air seemed deadly still.

I rocked from one foot to the other, in a vague hope that the movement might warm me. "Reverend, I really think I should get back to my B&B now. It's late, and it's ridiculously cold. I'm not going to get anything more—"

He held up a palm to quieten me and read from another page of print. This one seemed cleaner, not as aged as the others. I saw a brief flash of the headline as he unfolded it. A local magazine.

"In Dawlish, villagers saw the prints cross the length of the churchyard and wander between the graves. The tracks lead to the door of the vestibule, where they promptly disappeared. The cloven footprints remain a mystery, but many superstitious people in the village are afraid to go outside their doors after nightfall, particularly in the snowy, winter months."

I stuffed my notebook and pens into my satchel and slung it over my shoulder.

"Goodbye, Reverend. We'll talk more tomorrow. This was . . . interesting." I made for the door, but he side-stepped snake-fast and blocked my only exit.

"Do you have a camera in there?" he asked, nodding at my bag.

"I do," I admitted. "Why?" I heard a dull thud from somewhere in the chancel next door. "Is that Evelyn?" I asked, hopefully.

"I doubt it," the Reverend replied. "Get your camera ready, pull that silver cross out of your top, and follow me." He must have seen the reticence in my face. "Come on," he urged. "You want your story, don't you?"

He rummaged in his trouser pockets, and I saw a flash of metal in his hands. Something small with a keen, sharp edge. My stomach felt heavy with fear.

"Reverend, please . . ." I began, and heard the shake in my voice, but he spun away from me to face the wooden crucifix, mounted behind him on the wall.

"I've never asked you before, but I'm asking you now, let this be the end of it. Give me the strength that I need."

I stood dumbstruck for a moment before I realised; the Reverend wasn't talking to me.

More thumps, this time louder and from the body of the church. A repetitive boom, like a heartbeat. I heard taps on the glass as curved shapes cut the snow and *something* walked straight up the church wall.

Reverend Harrow rolled up his shirt sleeves and spread his arms wide like wings. He took a deep breath and grinned.

"You might not believe in the Devil," he said softly, "but the Devil believes in you."

ROUGH MUSIC

Die Booth

"And that was Morgan there, singing *My Way*, thank you Morgan!"

"Nice one, Morgan!"

Swaying a little, he navigated the steps down from the raised platform that served as a stage for karaoke. There was applause and tipsy shouts of support, but over the positive noise, all he could hear was Carl.

"Sounds like a turkey being slaughtered!"

Laughter: Morgan felt the hot, shivering adrenaline rush of anger as he re-joined the crowd, and then Carl was slapping him cheerfully across the back.

"Come on, Ol' Blue Eyes, before you upset the vegans. It's your round. Aw, mate . . ." Carl pulled a pouty face that made Morgan want to pummel him until he stopped speaking. "It's just bants. You know I'm only messing with you, right?"

"Right." Clenching his jaw until his back teeth squeaked, Morgan led the way to the bar.

*   *   *

He lost track of how many drinks later it was when the bell rang for closing time. There was late licence on a Friday, so it was likely past midnight. When he slipped out of a side door to avoid the usual kicking-out crowd—and more to the point, Carl—the alley was silent as fog. Cold as, too. Morgan regretted not wearing a coat. He pulled his red flannel shirt closed over his t-shirt as he started to weave towards the main street. If he was this drunk, he reasoned, and still shivering, then the weather must be icy. Yet the women waiting at the taxi rank were all merry in short dresses, the men in shirt sleeves. A cackle erupted from the queue that made Morgan wince: at the last moment, he veered off track, changing his course for one of the winding side-streets.

Walking home, he reasoned, would save money on a taxi fare, and give him time to sober up a bit so he didn't wake John when he got in. But when he heard the music, he couldn't help himself.

All he could make out was the muffled sound of drums, coming from inside one of the dark buildings that bordered the road. Perhaps it was the ale, dulling his reason, but something about the sound made him want to dance, and Morgan found himself rattling doorknobs and picking his way down a narrow side-passage in pursuit of the beat. It had to be a club. An after-hours speakeasy where he could get another drink, away from Carl or anyone else he knew, and end the night on a higher note.

He followed the sound down a steep set of stone steps, damp-slippery and reeking of bins. The door at the bottom stuck when he pushed it, the ancient wood swollen in the frame, but it was unlocked and let him in with an uncanny moan. It was dark inside. He stopped as the drums ceased and a match flared with a hiss, illuminating a figure perched on an old table, a strange round drum balanced in her lap.

"Sorry. I thought this was a club."

Leaning, she lit a candle. "That's alright. I like an audience." She started to play again, slower this time, pale fingers stroking the drum's pale skin like she was petting a cat. Morgan's feet itched. "You like it? It's a pear drum."

"What's a pear drum?"

The girl grinned, her fingers stilling once more. "This is. Want a go?"

The drum was lighter than he expected. It felt somehow alive, like holding a bird – airy and threatening flight. Morgan tapped it with a cautious fingertip. He broke into a smile. He'd always *known* that he was a natural musician—even without playing a drum before, his rhythm was flawless, the drum ringing out a mesmerising beat. "I love it." He could hardly bear to pass it back to the girl. "Where can I get one?"

"Oh. It's the only one." She cradled the drum, protectively. "But you can have it, if you do me a favour."

"What favour?"

Her green eyes glinted in the candle-fire. "You have to be bad."

"Ah. Sorry. I don't swing that way-" *Not to mention the fact you look barely eighteen.*

"Not that." The girl scoffed. "Here." She jumped silently down from the table, her footsteps making no noise as she approached and passed him a sealed white envelope. "Come back tomorrow."

"What does it—" When Morgan looked up from the envelope, she was gone.

* * *

The morning after, he woke at home on the couch with a thudding head, convinced of the strange dreams he'd had.

"Good night?" John asked, in *that* tone.

"Mmm." Morgan rubbed his face, and produced a creased envelope from his back pocket. "Carl was being a prick again."

"Babe. You shouldn't let him get to you." John handed him a cup of tea. His hand rested lightly on top of Morgan's hair, before he went back into the kitchen. Tearing open the envelope, Morgan pulled out a sheet of paper and read, in a neat inked hand:

Bring me the gnome from next door's garden.

How she knew about it, or why she wanted it, Morgan couldn't begin to fathom. Why he'd taken it, however, was quite clear to him, as he set the little plastic figure down on the table next to where the girl was lounging: he *wanted* that drum. She smiled, pleased, and stroked her fingers over the drum skin, with a noise like swishing fabric that made his blood yearn. He asked, "Can I have it?"

"Oh, you haven't been bad enough yet. You have to be badder. You have to be *really* bad." She handed him a new envelope. Inside was a note that read:

Piss through next door's letterbox.

Morgan's hand holding the note shook. He opened his mouth to speak, but didn't quite know what to say. When he glanced up to question her, she was gone again.

* * *

No matter how he tried to keep his eye on her over the following weeks, she still eluded him in the same way. If he completed a task, she'd be there with a newer, *worse* one, holding the drum like a trophy. A trophy he could win if only he just pushed that little bit further. If he went back without having completed his current task, it was to no avail: he searched the rotten old building and found only dust and mouse traps, she was never there, and nor was the drum, and he *wanted* it, with a feral obsession that vanquished all reason.

"You need to stop this." John said, when he caught him slashing the tyres of next door's car. "What are you *doing*?"

"I can't tell you." He couldn't. He wasn't even sure he knew himself. "But it's important."

"Is it more important than us?" John's voice was a sleety hiss, gaze flitting up and down the street. "Because if you carry on like this, we're done. I'll leave, and a new lover will come to live with you. With glass eyes and a wooden tail."

Morgan paused, sitting back on his heels to squint up at him. It was a stupid, nonsensical threat, but it was weirdly specific and it made him uneasy. "What the hell is that supposed to mean?"

"It means. . .you'll end up with the partner you deserve." John's stare settled, icy, on the vandalised tyre.

"I love you." Morgan said. "I'll stop." *I'll stop the moment I get that drum.*

* * *

It was a month to the day of first hearing the drum when Morgan crept down the stone steps, the sound of fire engine sirens still clanging in his skull. "Hello?" The scent of smoke clung to the back of his throat. He shone the flashlight of his phone around the dirty, empty room. The girl was nowhere to be seen, but the wide beam reflected off the polished bowl of the pear drum, and Morgan's heart samba'd.

* * *

The looks he got when he carried it onto the little stage at open mic were worth it when he began to play. It was *all* worth it. No matter how he struck the drum, the rhythm was perfectly toned and timed, entrancing and irresistible. The crowd were powerless. Clapping and calling, they danced. Not even his greatest karaoke performance could compare to the rush Morgan felt when he played the drum. He felt powerful. *Admired.* As he ended the song, the audience were already begging for more, and when he broke for a rest after his first set, people besieged him, offering pints and heaping praise. It wasn't just the beer he was drunk on. The flattery flowed, golden. As his foot lit upon the first step up to the stage, he saw the door open and Carl walked in. Morgan's chest swelled.

He leaned in to the mic. "This one's for Carl. Let's hope your dance moves are as good as my singing voice, eh, *mate?*"

As he started to play, Carl started to sway. Morgan smirked. His hands moved faster. Carl picked up pace. But the satisfying look of confusion on his face was quickly replaced with delight as he jumped along with the crowd.

"Morgan, mate, I gotta hand it to you. You can damn well play the drums! This is amazing!"

Morgan's hands faltered as Carl grinned, and twirled the girl dancing next to him—but the music merely changed direction again, as perfectly executed as before. Sure, Carl had complimented him. It had even sounded sincere. So why didn't it feel like a victory? Morgan watched from his solitary seat on the stage as Carl laughed and partied with his friends to the music of the drum. He hadn't expected him to look so *happy*.

That familiar tension was back, wiring his jaw. He hit the drum harder. And harder. As if he wanted to break it. But the drum only throbbed cheerfully beneath his thrashing hands, the rhythm picking up to a wild beat, sending the dancers whirling. The floor was a frenzy. At first people laughed, but soon they fell speechless and Morgan started to catch fleeting glimpses of distress on their faces as they whipped past, banging into tables and flailing their arms.

Carl didn't look quite so happy any more. "Come on, man, give it a rest!"

Morgan drummed faster. He began to cackle.

"Morgan, come on!"

The others in the crowd may as well have been invisible: all Morgan could see or hear was Carl; the rising panic in his voice, his face falling in fear.

"Morgan? Please?"

There it was. That grovelling little sob. Morgan laughed, until his sides ached and tears ran down his cheeks. Until he was shaking so hard with vicious mirth that he could no longer strike the drum and his audience slumped broken to the ground.

Nobody challenged him when he left the pub. They were scared—he was still carrying the drum, after all. As he stepped over exhausted bodies and out onto the night street, his feet felt light. It was a shame that he wouldn't be able to enjoy the adulation that came from playing there any more, but there were other pubs and other open mic nights, and after all, it was worth it to see Carl pay.

* * *

When he arrived home, he was in good spirits. Fishing his keys from his pocket, he juggled the drum beneath his arm as he went to unlock the door, only for it to swing gently open at his touch. A whisper of chill caressed the nape of his neck, and he caught the whiff of soot drifting from next door. It was dark inside the house, and that darkness seemed familiar.

"John?"

No answer. Morgan peered into the hallway, but some reluctance kept him from stepping over the threshold.

"John?"

Nothing. Except . . . from within the house, an odd noise, like the *thud, thud, thud* of wood on tile.

"John, are you in there?"

Thump, thump – muffled now, as if on carpet. Whatever was in there was moving around. Morgan retreated a step. Flattening his back against the wall, he peered through the blinds of the front window. There were no lights on, but in the blue glow of the TV set he could see the inhuman glint of glass eyes, and through the window he could hear the steady thump of a wooden tail.

BLACK HOLE CASTLE

Lorraine Schein

The astronaut fell into the black hole castle.
    Its walls were slick with sticky menstrual blood
    that smeared the visor of her space helmet.
    The event horizon stairs spiraled to a madwoman in the attic
    who was screaming, who was her.
    Ghosts of other women astronauts haunted it.
    They had fallen in from other failed missions
    and exploded rockets like the Challenger.
    Christa's dismembered pulped body parts and face remnants
    floated around her like ectoplasmic meteor shards.
    The lord of this grand empty manor was like Bluebeard,
    but supermassive.
    He wanted to eat her, suck her into oblivion.
    He gave the astronaut a key, but told her to never use it.
    The key was a severed index finger,
    veins hanging from it like red comets' tails.
    It could not unlock any door—there were no doors,
    no rooms to open.
    The only escape was to spew out through a white hole
    and run run run screaming
    into a new universe where a man could maybe save her.

LAST MEAL

Angela Sylvaine

This malignant heart draws me toward
    those anguished, not taking life but
    syphoning sorrow to feed my dark gluttony
    while the winged reaper works
    Nestled in the room's corner, perched on gloom's
    skeletal finger with watchful orbs a shining beacon
    of death, the Owl's feathers waft sweet rot
    No more just morbid observer, I wait my turn
    for the bird of prey to collect
    I latched windows, locked doors, but this
    ancient became mist to slip through seams
    Feathers rustle, the hollow quills housing mites
    that nibble, too, feeding on that which eats demise
    He coos a warning, the soft trill drawing
    rank sweat from my scalding skin
    The last a broken boy, not yet gone,
    but I didn't call for help, just smiled
    at the hoot and turn of the mighty bird's head,
    the hook of his beak an arrow piercing the
    boy's chest to hook a glittering scrap of
    soul, a wet and wriggling worm, before
    pinning me with his harbinger's stare
    A screech splits my ears, fills canals with hot
    blood that drips, stains my sheet, my shroud

Talons grip cotton and flesh, eyes circled
with the fingernails of ghosts bore, reflect,
a mirror for my sins, promising payment
Death's mantle, gorged, crushes spiderweb
cracked ribs, ensures each breath is agony
His hooked maw opens but doesn't eat the tainted,
instead spewing a pellet into my gaping mouth
I gasp, suck in dusty moth wings and wiry fur,
cough against the dry mass that cracks,
expands, shards of black beetle shell and stripped
white pin bones piercing my tender throat
I thrash and cry, choking on a last meal of recompense

CUL-DE-SAC

Stephanie Rabig

"Get your nose out of that book and go play! Honestly, when I was your age, kids did things instead of just reading about them. You have—"

"Okay," Caleb said, bouncing off his bed, leaving his book open for later.

". . . oh," his mother said, used to lecturing him for at least five more minutes before he agreed to leave the sanctuary of his room.

He wasn't about to explain, but it was because his Dad was due home any minute and he and Mom were watching new episodes of some cop show. He didn't mind when they watched reruns, because they were both pretty quiet. But new episodes of anything meant that Mom was pausing literally every minute or two to comment on something a character said, or asking Dad if he thought so-and-so was the killer, or talking about what actual case may have inspired the episode, until Dad finally snapped, "Would you shut the fuck up and watch already?" and then Mom would get pissed and the show would play on, unnoticed, while they argued.

Bartholomew would tease him by saying it was their way of flirting. Whether it was or not, it always gave him a headache.

Caleb ran to the other end of the cul-de-sac and rang Bartholomew's doorbell, tapping his foot and twisting his fidget ring around and around while he waited for him to answer the door.

His best friend's mom answered instead, smiling down at him. "Hey, Caleb. He's out back."

"Thanks, Mrs. Whitaker!" He charged around back and opened the gate, careful not to let their golden retriever, Sandy, out as he slipped inside.

Bartholomew was playing with his toy dinosaurs, sitting in the freshly-cut grass. It made Caleb's nose itch just looking at him.

Alerted to his presence by Sandy's barks, Bartholomew looked up and grinned. "You wanna play?"

"Sure!" He'd take an allergy pill when he got home. "But first we gotta ask your mom if you can stay over tonight."

"Okay!" He got up, and then saw the way Caleb was rapidly leaning from foot to foot, the way he did when he was excited. "What's up?"

Caleb thought about waiting, but the thought disappeared almost before it formed. He'd already waited a whole entire week.

"I saw a dinosaur!"

"What?" Bartholomew asked, his expression hesitant, and Caleb knew he was trying to figure out whether he was pulling a prank or not.

"It was one of those long-necked ones. What do you call it, a pleistocene?"

"Pleistocene is the name of an era," Bartholomew corrected. "Do you mean plesiosaurus?"

"Yeah, that's it! I saw it a week ago, and I thought I was dreaming, and—"

"Wait, wait. You saw a dinosaur a week ago and you're only telling me *now*?"

"I wanted to make really sure! So I've stayed up late every night this week, and every night I've seen her, at exactly three minutes past three. So you have to stay over!"

Bartholomew still looked a little sceptical, but the excitement won out, and he charged into the house, calling for his mom.

"Okay," he said as he leaned back outside. "I can stay! I've gotta figure out what to pack. I need my binoculars, and my camera, and I can sneak one of my brother's energy drinks if we're gonna stay up *that* late, and my good colored pencils for notes and a drawing of it, and . . ."

He continued rattling things off, and Caleb laughed. "Do you want to just move in for the night?"

"If you seriously saw a dinosaur, heck yeah I'm moving in."

The suggestion he might be making it up stung a little, but not enough for him to say anything. He'd see it too, soon.

"Bartholomew, shut the door! I'm not trying to air condition the outside!"

He sheepishly closed the door, and Caleb waited for him to gather what turned out to be an enormous duffle bag full of stuff.

"Let's just drop your stuff off and then play outside for a while," Caleb said. "Mom and dad are watching *new episodes*."

Bartholomew winced, and the two boys hurried into Caleb's house, dropped the bag on the bed, and then ran back out again.

"Tell me everything," Bartholomew said. "Where did you see it?"

"Right here!" Caleb said, pointing to the dark pavement of the cul-de-sac. "My window faces the street, right, and I woke up and got a drink of water and I thought I saw something move outside, so I turned off my nightlight and looked out and she was swimming, right here."

"In . . . in the pavement?" Bartholomew said, moving a foot off the sidewalk and experimentally toeing at the asphalt.

"Yeah!"

"And you've seen her every night this week?"

"Swear to God," he said, holding up three fingers like he'd seen people do on TV.

Bartholomew looked more skeptical than excited now, and Caleb resisted the urge to roll his eyes. "Whatever. You'll see. C'mon, let's go get some candy."

* * *

After a visit to the nearest convenience store, a brief lecture from Caleb's father about spending all his allowance on junk food, a (futile) beg-a-thon to order pizza for dinner, and almost three hours playing video games, it was finally time for bed.

They had the light off and were pretending to be asleep at 11:00, when his Mom and Dad always came in to check on him. As soon as the door shut again, they sprang up and back to their phones, watching YouTube videos.

At 1:30, despite the energy drink he'd been sipping on, Bartholomew started to droop.

Caleb tried to keep him awake, but finally decided it'd be less stressful to just let him sleep and wake him up at close to 3:00.

After an hour and a half (that felt more like six hours) Caleb shook his friend awake. Bartholomew grumbled and swatted at him, but when Caleb said the magic word—*dinosaur*—his friend remembered what he was here for and scrambled to the window.

"Where is it?"

"Two more minutes," Caleb said, his nose pressed to the window. "Hey! Phone off! The light's gonna keep us from seeing out."

"But I want to get a video!"

"We can go outside and get one."

"This late?" Bartholomew asked, and Caleb rolled his eyes.

"Don't be a wuss."

"I'm not a wuss! I just don't want to get in . . ."

He trailed off, dropping his phone as he stared slack-jawed out the window.

"I told you," Caleb whispered.

The black asphalt looked like a round, glassy pond in the moonlight. As they stared, an enormous animal surfaced, head breaching for a few short seconds, stretching toward the stars before diving, elongated body sinking beneath the water.

"What are you doing up this late?"

In an instant, the dinosaur was gone as his mother flipped on the light.

"Mom!" Caleb groaned.

"Don't you '*mom*' me! It is three in the morning!"

"There . . . there was a dinosaur," Bartholomew whispered.

"Oh, Bart, you just had a nightmare," his mom said, not registering how Bartholomew gritted his teeth at the nickname. Kids had taunted him with Simpsons jokes for years; he hated it when people didn't use his full name.

"Yeah," he grumbled. "Guess so."

"C'mon, get back to bed. No phones, either."

The moment she was gone, they were both at the window again, but the dinosaur had disappeared.

* * *

The next night, Bartholomew had no trouble staying up.

"And you're sure it's stayed around longer before?" he asked, scribbling in his notebook.

"Yeah. The first night I saw her, when she left and I went to bed it was almost five a.m."

"It might have something to do with an adult being here," Bartholomew mused. "In which case, it could react the same way to being filmed. I won't take out my phone right away."

"Good." Caleb grinned. "I do think we should go outside, though."

". . . really?"

"Yeah! Imagine being right up close to her!"

"Imagine her thinking we're food."

* * *

At 3:02, one minute before their dinosaur was scheduled to show up, they crept out the front door.

"Look," Caleb whispered, as the asphalt in front of them rippled.

As if in a trance, Bartholomew moved forward, stretching his hand out. He crouched on the sidewalk and experimentally tapped the asphalt. His hand sank through.

"It's water," he whispered, reverent. "Come here. It's water."

Caleb hurried forward, dipping his foot in, barely holding back a laugh. "Wow."

"There she is."

Caleb looked up, watching as the plesiosaurus swam, twisting and turning around in the lake of their once-boring cul-de-sac.

When it resurfaced, it was closer, and he was torn between a cautious step back or a fascinated step forward.

Bartholomew had no such compunctions; he stepped forward, teetering on the edge of the sidewalk. Then he held out his hand.

"Hey!" Caleb hissed, half-afraid his voice would break the spell, also counting on it. Bartholomew had joked earlier about it thinking they were food, and they'd both laughed, but now it didn't seem funny at all.

The animal stretched its elongated neck, staring down at them with green eyes that reminded Caleb of a crocodile's, before bumping its nose against Bartholomew's hand and nearly knocking him over.

Bartholomew laughed, a high-pitched sound that was equal parts awe and hysteria. "I pet her, Caleb! I *pet* a *dinosaur*."

Emboldened, Caleb stretched out his own hand. The plesiosaurus bumped against it, making a low rumbling sound deep in its chest that Caleb really hoped meant *hello, new friend* and not *you might be tasty.*

"C'mere, girl," Bartholomew said, leaning forward, hand outstretched, on his tiptoes on the very edge of the curb. Caleb reached for him, his fingers only succeeding in brushing against his shirtsleeve before Bartholomew fell in.

"Shit!" Caleb cried, crouching down and waving his hands around under the water, trying to grab his friend's hand.

He didn't feel anything.

Could Bartholomew even swim? How deep was this?

Had to be really, really deep, he thought, to hold their dinosaur.

"Fuck shit goddammit," Caleb whispered, the thrill of saying so many forbidden words in a row not even touching his panic. If they'd planned on going in, they would've brought the old lasso he had up in his room, would have tied it to the street sign and then around their waists.

But he didn't have time to get it now. Bartholomew wasn't coming back up.

He pinched his nose shut and looked up at their dinosaur. She was watching him, her head tilted, and he was reminded of curious birds inspecting a new type of food in their feeder.

"Please don't eat me," he muttered, his voice nasal because of his blocked-off nose, and then he drew in a deep breath and stepped forward into the water.

He plummeted. The knowledge that this lake wasn't natural at all, that it might keep going and going to the end of the universe, nearly made him suck in a panicked breath.

Instead, he opened his eyes. The water didn't sting the way the stuff at the local pool did, but he still couldn't see very well.

If Bartholomew wasn't flailing around like—well, like a panicking kid in too-deep water—he never would've seen him.

He swam forward, grabbing hold of Bartholomew and nearly catching a fist to the nose for his trouble before his friend realized it was him. Caleb kicked for the surface, nearly running out of air before he finally reached it. Bartholomew had gone limp in his arms, and he pushed him partly up onto the sidewalk, treading water and coughing.

"Caleb! Bartholomew!"

"Mom, no—!"

The flashlight beam sliced through the dark, and Caleb's mother caught a glimpse of a nightmare scene: her son sunk most of the way into the pavement, which was rippling like water around him. His friend, lying half-in and half-out of the water, unconscious at best. And overlooking them both was a creature out of a nightmare, neck stretched high and lips peeled back from enormous, sharp teeth.

She screamed, and then her husband was beside her, his flashlight beam joining hers and revealing what was actually there.

No monster. No impossible water.

Just Caleb and Bartholomew. Bartholomew cut in half at the waist, and her son's decapitated head slowly rolling forward, coming to rest in the gutter next to the body of his friend.

THE LONELINESS OF MALABRON

Basile Lebret

Picture a bathroom. The place is ten by ten feet wide. Entering, the toilet sits on your left. Bathtub is across the room from the door. It takes up almost the entirety of the wall thanks to an add-on table made of tiles which lays by the head of it. The tenants adorned it with towels.

Picture the bathtub, its entire complexity. Stepping in, as you sit inside a sad shade of blue you notice that on the left flank exists a burn mark. Remnants of a teenager once having inhabited the abode. The new occupants don't know the minute details of this scar, promised themselves they would ditch the whole thing, forget. Sometimes, on a really slow day, Cléo's skin will touch upon the blotched plastic, she will shiver and promise herself to change the whole apparatus.

Picture the sharp coldness which bites as you sit naked on the sea-coloured polymer. There is no water yet. Picture the loneliness and the frailty. Picture the vulnerability. As you're laying there, vivid landscapes flash across your eyelids. Cyclopean castles, sharp towers and tight loopholes. Some nude, hairy peasants, others wearing robes, trying to wash themselves. Anguished cats and the pungent smell of faeces. You don't want to sit among the breezing flanks.

Picture Malabron. All scarlet pupils and moist pelage and curved claws and artificially sharpened dentition. You cannot picture the entirety of the entity; for if you stare at it for too long, the image of a white horse running amok forms in your mind. The avatar does not replace the previous form, it just stacks upon it. Then comes a salmon big enough to gulp whole fleets in its powerful mouth, devoid of teeth. All three apparitions stack and somehow fit and do not fit in the bathtub. No one ever talks of the fourth iteration. Leave it at that.

Picture the house. Building is pink and warm-looking and easy on the eyes. Garden used to be a mess but is now slowly growing back into a hospitable shape under Aurore's expert hand. In here, in France, some would say *her green hand*. Cléo liked this den, her wife had her doubts but the flourishing exterior Aurore was able to build, all by herself, shut even the more abrasive of those.

Picture the couple. Cléo is petite and tanned and brunette. Aurore is slightly taller, lean and blonde. The former is a dentist, renting an office two towns away. Aurore is more grounded; she works in Human Resources when she's not gardening.

Picture Malabron in the bathtub, shrinking as people lose their belief in old folk tales. Imagine the faery wondering what will become of him in a world of smartphones and satellites and sponge vertebrae carrying 4K signals. Picture the cold flanks made of stiffened petroleum, the artificial but very real solitude. There exist deep harsh nights on which the creature lets the water pour in and then swims and swims and swims. In a circle. The bathtub, his entire world. No one notices. Even the water bill can't prove Malabron's existence.

Moons ago, a relative of Cléo stumbled upon the faery's dance macabre. Picture the scream. Picture the muffled whoosh of the towel hitting the tiled floor. Picture the sapphic couple's embarrassment when faced with an empty bathtub full of lukewarm water. Howling sibling left without turning back, assured the couple she would never step foot under their roof for as long as they'd be living there. Both Cléo and Aurore felt relieved. They never talked about it. Picture your last contact with anyone being a shrieking escape.

You cannot picture the fights, the sleepless nights, the endless discussions. Cléo wants a baby, Aurore wants a baby. Both wish their offspring could come from their own womb. Yet, with them being lesbians, and living in France, said child would never be the official son or daughter of their partner. He or she would need to be adopted; which could lead to a legal battle in case the worst happened to the natural parent.

Picture Cléo's parents being homophobes. Picture the cold walks outside and the screams and the insults. Picture the adult who forced you into this world hating you for no discernible reason. Picture your genitor despising your loved one.

The women, they settle on Aurore bearing their first born. Picture Cléo's heart only half-broken. Picture the research and the trip to Spain and the appointments. Picture Aurore's shitty Spanish accent. Picture Cléo's sincere smile. Swelling belly, swelling feet. Aurore trying to maintain her garden while being double her regular size. Picture Cléo, half worried, half proud, looking at her other half through a frost-bitten window.

Picture the infant. He is tiny and warm and if you get close enough you can smell the musk of Aurore upon him. The parents, they name him Bastien. He is the most beautiful boy the couple has ever seen. Cléo was afraid she would be sad, oddly jealous. She is not. The mother worries that her progeny could get hurt somehow.

A small part of the brunette is happy Aurore finally put on some weight. Yet, there is little to no doubt soon the blonde will regain her past figure, she already is. Cléo can't help but think Aurore's success regaining her silhouette means Cléo failed to keep hers. Aurore would not even think such a thing. Aurore would never let her wife feel this way.

Picture the baby's room. It's vast and pastel, full of blue and rose. Cléo wanted it blue but Aurore often has the last word. The baby is fine and dandy there. Sometimes, late at night, Malabron comes and recounts tales.

The faery speaks of arcane princesses who webbed sand castles into the firmament, of secrets which smell like the moon when she witnesses blood loss. The entity knows which stars to whisper to in order to bless the child. He sometimes does. Only his first form reflects on the cornea of the little human's eye. The infant is not scared. The child doesn't run. The child does not shriek.

Picture the old being teaching the baby how to summon a hellhound with only a rabbit and oak moss. Picture the beast revealing, through a tongue long dead, which angels to call upon if equipped with an Agrippa. Monster says only the east. All the others are conmen. The monster tells the baby he once met King Arthur, and scientists wondering if he ever existed do not matter. Faery complains. Picture Cléo wondering why her infant's room sometimes smells like dog fur and unmoving water.

With the previous tenants, Malabron used to play tricks. He's the one who set the mattress on fire while the prodigal son was busy smoking weed. Boy tried to extinguish the blaze by fitting the whole thing into the bathtub, dampened it, forgot about it, went back, saw it was burning still and really extinguished it this last time. The Korrigan was there a lifetime ago, when a twelve-year old boy walked into the brightly lit kitchen only to discover his mom, laying on the floor, having had a seizure. Ambulance could not make it in time to the nearest hospital. The monster does not tell it to Bastien, yet he thinks the mother stared at him for far too long. Doctors said aneurysm. This diagnostic made the beast laugh.

Picture the boy still thinking to this day he killed his own mother when he was in grade school. Picture the adult who drinks.

Malabron was also there when Aurore doubted and brought her ex and they had sex and the girl hovered above him for the longest time trying to wash away the shame and the sin and the unease. The monster can, still now, picture the other woman's dark skin.

Picture the loneliness of Malabron inside of the bathtub's cold, cold flanks. Picture his joy of having someone able to see him again. Seeing is all that matters. Bastien is young enough he can witness and read and hear the whole of the faery. The babe, he trusts the creature for it comes on most nights.

Hence why the son does not cry on this peculiar witching hour when Malabron extracts him from his blue crib, overhead the mobile swings and makes just a tiny noise. The fae is gentle. His grip is firm for he cares very much about the baby. Bastien is not sufficiently aware that he could see Malabron's fourth form. Picture Malabron pouring water into the tub as the child stares at him, seated upon the toilet. The boy, he does not fall.

Picture Malabron checking with its scaly fingers if the liquid is warm enough. Picture Malabron happy as he smiles and scoops up the baby boy. Picture Malabron bringing Aurore and Cléo's son into his deepest trenches.

There is a sea in the bathtub. A cobalt sky lays there in wait over a blue ocean that seems to never end. Although, from yours or the child's perspective those unseen bounds appear to blur between overstretching sea and walls of calcified petroleum. Wait there long enough and you'll hear the rumble. It is slow at first but there are no waves inbound. As the rush progresses closer you can feel it in your bones this is no ordinary current. Picture the blind fish.

Picture the lone house on the next morning. It's pink and somehow welcoming. The garden appears in good shape but can still be worked upon. Picture the piercing scream. And the sobs. A door slamming shut. Another cry. Picture the small body underneath the water.

IN THE WOODS, SOMEWHERE

Maxx Fidalgo

"I still don't think this is a good idea."

"Would you shut up? This is the only way! Or do you want to lose your job? We get fired now, it'll take us forever to find another gig," Tyson said. There was an ever-present tinge of anger to his voice when he spoke and a wrinkle between his brows from frowning so much. His blond head only came up to his companion's shoulder and he told himself every day that it didn't bother him.

It did.

"We're young!" Nate insisted. The young man wrung his hands, blowing a lock of dark hair from his eyes. Nate was tall and fit, a regular jock if not for the fact that he gravitated to anyone who could tell him what to do and how to do it. There was a stoop in his shoulders, from ducking his head and never making eye contact with anyone. "We're kids, okay? This is . . . this is kinda crazy, man." He peeked into the restaurant. Technically, he and Tyson were off from work today. But they had stopped by the upscale, family-owned restaurant they worked at in Middleborough to say hello to their boss's new baby and to drop a capful of antifreeze into their coworker's soda cup.

"You think lives can't be destroyed at sixteen?" Tyson snorted, peeking around the doorframe to spy on their coworker, Micah, again. He was bussing dishes today, cowlicked brown hair in his face and smiling nicely at everyone as he ran around from table to table, like he wasn't tired, or actually *liked* what he was doing. Tyson shook his head and turned back to Nate, out of sight. It wouldn't do for Micah to know they were here. He might get suspicious. After all, he was out to get them, wasn't he?

"I'm seventeen," Nate said. He cast a furtive glance at Micah as the young man ran by, catching sight of a waitress starting to clear her own table. He quickly took over, running cups to the bar, throwing a smile at everyone he passed. Nate frowned. The owners had recently trained Micah as a bar-back too, which was *Nate's* job. And Tyson had been bussing for *months* before Micah had shown up and wowed everyone with his dedication and likeability.

"Whatever," said Tyson. "It'll be fine. He'll be gone, they'll wonder what happened, and in that time, we stake our claim. By the time he finds his way back here, no one will want to give him a job."

"He's the boss's cousin," Nate muttered.

"So what, it's nepotism?" Tyson ran his hands through his fair hair, pulling at it in frustration. "Look, he's already taken the servers' and bartenders' complaints to the boss. At this rate, he'll have our jobs and we'll have nothing!"

"Well, we don't do much, man," Nate replied softly. Sure they slacked off and cut corners, but they were young. Micah was twenty-two and had a work ethic. Plus, he had student loans to pay off, and that was as good a motivator as any.

"Then go home, Nate," Tyson said with a sneer. "Lose it all; I'm not doing this for you."

Nate crossed his arms and paced a bit, not leaving. He missed the small smile that flit across Tyson's face; Tyson had known Nate wouldn't leave. Nate may have been older, but he had no sense of direction and was far too easy to manipulate. It hadn't taken much convincing to get him to dump the antifreeze into Micah's cup. The solution was sweet, so Micah wouldn't taste it or realize anything was wrong until it was too late. The young man always chugged down a soda before he left the restaurant for home.

Tyson and Nate sat in the darkened function room until Micah was let off from his shift around 9:30 PM. Already he was making faces and rubbing his stomach in discomfort. Tyson watched him go and then led Nate out to the darkened parking lot where they found Micah lying unconscious by his car. Tyson took Micah's car keys off his body and unlocked the trunk. When he turned, Nate was still standing there, staring.

"What are you waiting for? Pick him up and stuff him in!" Tyson yelled.

"Shut up!" Nate hissed, looking around with wide-eyed fear. But there was no one around in the darkened night. The town was small and in a rural part of southern Massachusetts where curfews were adhered to and no one was out after nightfall. "What are we going to do with him?"

"One of my friends recommended this guy. He lives near the woods in Lakeville. He said he'd take anything you bring him. Drugs, stolen merch, people. . . he'll make Micah disappear for a while." Tyson bent down and grabbed Micah's legs. "Now grab the rest of him and help me."

Together, they crammed Micah in the trunk and got into his car. Tyson drove as Nate sat in the passenger seat, drumming his fingers on his knee and craning his neck to look out the back window.

"Stop that," Tyson said, eyes locked on the road. "No one saw us, no one knew we were going to try anything. You're making me nervous, so stop it."

Nate forced himself to look at the road instead, hands squeezed together in his lap.

Middleborough was close enough to the Lakeville woods that it only took ten minutes to get to their destination. It was more rural than Middleborough, with houses so spaced apart the nearest neighbor was half a mile away, separated by dense, sprawling woods and silent, eerie lakes that drained into gnarled swamps. By then, the night had grown pitch black, the lack of streetlights on the backroads throwing everything into darkness. A dirt road, pitted with stones and holes, led deeper into the trees that grew larger and made the woods denser the further in you went.

"I . . . I don't think we can fit," Nate said. "The road's a mess. The car could pop a tire." Maybe they could ditch the car before Micah woke up and get away with this fiasco. Maybe the fear of waking up in his own trunk in the woods would be enough.

"It's not our car," Tyson said with a shrug, turning on the high beams and driving forward. He would shut them off once they got to the meeting place, so as not to be too suspicious. He didn't need any curious neighbors or wandering police officers to see a light on amid the trees and run in to investigate. They would be fine, as long as Nate continued to listen.

Bump, bump, bump they went, into the woods, into the dark, somewhere beyond. Nate shook quietly in his seat and swallowed back tears. Tyson drove on, fighting any apprehension that built in his gut. They reached an end to the road five minutes later, and Tyson abruptly cut the engine, causing Nate to jump.

"Get your shit together, man," Tyson said. "The guy always shows up at midnight in case people want to bring him something. So we wait, we dump the body, and we go. We never have to hear from him again. And we pretend this never happened."

"Isn't this too much? Tyson, isn't this—I mean. That's a *person*, isn't this—"

"Well, what are you gonna do now, huh?" Tyson laughed, the sound cruel and hard. "Run away? You can't find your way home and *you* put the antifreeze in his cup. What would happen if I went to the cops? Who's gonna believe it *wasn't* the older kid's idea?"

"You—you wouldn't!" Nate shouted. What had he done? What had he agreed to, getting into this with Tyson?

Tyson stared at the dark past the windshield. "Try me."

They sat and waited for the next few hours, Tyson tapping his thumbs against the steering wheel and Nate staring at his hands in a state of desolation beside him. Eventually, Tyson's phone alarm chirped. It was midnight. Neither boy could see anything in the woods before them, but Tyson got out of the car anyway.

"Let's go," he barked, and Nate scrambled out the passenger side after him.

Everything was dark. There was a crescent moon with not enough light, only a few stars. The trees were just another shade of black against the night, but between them, something shifted, caught the faint moonlight. A flash of grey stone in points, a flutter of ripped black fabric, something decomposing, soupy, and purple-black underneath. Nate panted in fear. Tyson swallowed, faltering.

"Hey, you the man?" he yelled. The figure must have been seven feet tall, that grey stone on its head spiking up toward the trees. Tyson steadied himself, rage burning through him. He just wanted this to be over with. "We've got something for you."

What have you brought me?

A nudge, at the back of their brains. A slither. A whisper.

Tyson shivered. He wasn't surprised to feel Nate's fingers tightening on his arm.

"What the *hell* was that Tyson, *what the hell was that?*" Nate blathered, squeezing Tyson's arm tighter.

"A body," Tyson answered, ignoring Nate.

Maybe it was the wrong answer. Even worse, the right one. In the dark, the figure shifted. The wind died. Not a leaf shook. The moon, Tyson realized, was gone. There were no stars. And everything was quiet.

Show me.

"Tyson—"

"Help me carry him," Tyson gritted out through clenched teeth. He pressed the button on the car fob and popped the trunk. This man, whoever he was, was freaking Tyson out. It wasn't right, whatever was in the dark. And where had the moon gone? Tyson could have sworn there was a nail-clipping moon out tonight.

They looked in the trunk. It was empty.

"Tyson. *Tyson!*" Nate fell against the car.

"Where did he . . ." Tyson stared at the darker shade of black that was the inside of the trunk. His heart fluttered in his throat.

"Did we—did we imagine it? Did we imagine it?" Nate turned to Tyson, almost unrecognizable in the dark. "Are you *screwing* with me? Was this some prank you two pulled? What the *hell* is going on?"

"I don't know!" Tyson slammed the trunk shut and walked around the car, toward the flickering shadow between the trees. There was something new beside it, another figure. Behind them, in the distance, a large grey tree rose up from the ground. Tyson could see it in the dark. He didn't understand how. "What's the deal? What's going on?" he yelled, voice shaking. This had to be a joke. Micah had suspected, maybe, and was messing with them. Something. Anything.

There's a man in the woods, shrouded in a swath of darkness, a shawl of leaves. He wears a stone moose skull as a mask–or is it?–with a booming voice, but smooth like top-shelf whiskey, like the devil in your dreams, coming from everywhere, until suddenly it's whispering right by your ear, telling you everything you don't want to hear.

"Who is that?" Nate said, running up beside Tyson. Nate pointed to the second figure, walking closer to them in the dark, stiff and jerky, a puppet on drunken strings. "Tyson. Who is that?"

"I don't - I don't know . . ." Tyson watched as it came closer and closer. Their hair flipped in a cowlick at the front of their head.

Micah stopped a foot away from them.

It *was* Micah, in shades of grey in the darkness, like all the color had been sucked from him. When he stared, it was with eyes that shone like the glass eyes of a doll, no spark of light or life behind them. Even now, he was still smiling and it wasn't so nice anymore. At first, just the automatic flex of facial muscles, the stretch and pull of skin. But then, gradually, it turned more sinister with those dead eyes staring straight ahead.

There's a man in the woods—but is he a man, really?—and he doesn't want your soul, no, he wants you, *in all your imperfect, messy, mortal glory of blood and flesh and bone. He can't do much with a soul and you're perfectly useful without it. But he'll take it all, sell it to someone else who can and will make better use of it while he uses* you.

"I. Have. Two. Bodies. For. You," Micah's voice said somewhere behind his body. The smiling mouth did not move. There were red leaves in his hair, stuffed under his scalp, wilting out of his ears, shiny and wet. The horned figure behind him shifted between the trees.

"What does he—what what does he mean, Tyson?" Nate was crying. "Tyson, I'm scared. Tyson!"

"Where's the moon?" Tyson asked, voice soft. He looked up to the sky.

Nate moaned. There was no light. But they could see. Around them, more figures appeared, coming up from the ground at the base of that grey tree. They jerked and swung about, limbs flailing. The heavy scent of rot hung in the air with them, mixed with the spicy stench of dead leaves. Nate started to tug at Tyson's hand, trying to drag him back to Micah's car.

Micah stood there, still smiling. Then his mouth dropped open in a silent scream, and he retched icy blue antifreeze onto the ground at their feet.

Nate screamed.

Tyson couldn't move.

"Tyson, Tyson, let's just go, please, okay? *Okay!*"

"Nate, where's the moon?"

"I don't care about the moon, let's *go.*" Nate tugged on Tyson's arm. Between the trees, the horned figure in the swirling cloak shifted its head toward them. Nate felt unseen eyes watching him, felt hands around his wrists and joints and neck.

Two bodies, it said. But the voice came out of Tyson's mouth. Nate let go of him and yelped.

There's a man in the woods—

"He's not a man, he's not a man, Tyson, snap out of it, he's not a man!"

There's a man in the woods—

"Tyson, give me the keys. Give me the keys and run, *run!*"

There's a man in the woods—

"Tyson, the car it's - where's the car? Please, please, no! *Run!*"

There's a man in the woods—

"Oh god—"

There's no god here.

"They're screaming, can't you hear them screaming? Get away, don't touch me! *Tyson!*"

There's a Man in the Woods. And he's coming for you.

* * *

An officer heading home on the backstreets of Lakeville pulled over to a dark figure on the side of the road. He was a young man, maybe twenty-one or twenty-two. He had cowlicked hair and the most pleasant smile as he emerged from the woods.

"You alright?" she asked through a rolled-down window.

"Think I can get a ride home, officer?" Micah asked with a warm grin. "I think someone pranked me and moved my car."

He didn't live far from the woods, just a mile down the road. She let him out and watched until he had made it inside the little, rundown house. Then she drove away, shivering, back past the dark trees she had found him near.

Later, she would tell her wife that just before she found him there, she swore she heard screaming in the woods, somewhere.

* * *

It took three days for the missing posters to go up, so long a demigod could have died and risen in the same amount of time. There were two boys with smiling faces, their pictures pulled from social media. The older one had dark hair and a shy smile; the younger one fair haired with his chest puffed out in confidence.

Micah's cousin sat at the restaurant's bar, staring at a copy of the poster on the counter top, long after the doors had been closed to their patrons. Her husband had taken their baby home when she had volunteered to stay and help close for the night. Behind the bar, Micah methodically polished glasses and lined them up in neat rows.

Outside, it was so dark there was only a wall of black beyond their windows.

Outside, something moved between the trees.

"Where *are* they?" she asked, voice fearful and tremulous, but not surprised. Outside, it got impossibly darker. The only sound was of the wind-rattled leaves. "Micah?"

His head snapped up as if pulled by a string. His eyes shone like the glass eyes of a doll, with no spark of light or life behind them. With a voice like the groaning wind, or moaning dead, he responded, "Are? They aren't anywhere. They aren't anything. Not any more."

He turned his back to her and continued polishing the glass.

MOTHER; MICROBES

H.V. Patterson

We are the microbes that ate your Mother;
    we are what she became.
    Lost at sea, drowning then dead,
    her last thought was you, daughter.
    Her bones so soft and fragile
    we cradled them and fed like
    a child feeds from a mother. We felt
    you, her daughter, our daughter now,
    your DNA imprinted inside
    her very marrow
    We pulled memories
    from calcium and phosphate.
    We knew you, and loved you
    drenched in sunlight, hair corona flame around your head,
    though we didn't yet know "head" or "sun" or "flame"
    and had no "eyes" to see.
    Still, we knew,
    ingested love with your mother's bones
    Lovesick for you, we crept from the depths.
    It was lifetimes, generations dead and dying,
    breathing poisonous air, but
    as we divided, we passed along the memories:
    her bones, her love.
    You were our first awareness,

first understanding of hands
and grasping,
of pain
and yearning
We were your shelter, your milk, your Mother;
we will be your home once more
Why run from us?
We felt your feet-flutter, heard your scream
as you emerged from amniotic sea
to this oxygen-drowned world.
Now, we have come to take you back
to the loving depths
and slow, deep currents.
We have come, our daughter, to hold you
close, to take each fragment of you,
eyes like pearl, lips like coral, teeth cutting as shell,
your bones and their marrow,
within us
Then we will return
to the cold, dark waters and be, eternally,
Mother and daughter.
Trillions of hungry bodies, a million generations,
thriving in the crushing dark.
Loving and loved
even after the sun goes out.

REGRETFULLY,

Maija Haavisto

they are not wanted
    yet they enter noisily
    through the flap in the door
    that was made for them
    though we'd rather
    tape that ugly mouth shut
    some claim humans have
    no natural predators
    but we all know what they are:
    venomous envelopes
    the words yes, no, please
    "Regretfully"
    "Yours sincerely"
    the prey animal enters
    a state of tonic immobility
    to ward off the fangs
    of *Yours sincerely*
    but regretfully, a fake death
    is rarely a useful strategy
    with these beasts
    you may take out the trash
    but that thing has laid eggs already
    it photocopied its signature
    in the white space, the spot where

it stings the most

ASLEEP AFIRE

Sam Lesek

Incendiary;
    A match is struck
    in the shape of a bone-white cigarette,
    an armchair sleep,
    and a secret ember
    hidden in her guts.
    Asleep, her wax
    begins to crackle and catch,
    feverish heat blanketing her,
    bellyfuls of sedative kindling
    ensuring inflammation.
    Dragon-like, the blaze
    flicks like a forked tongue
    between teeth and maw,
    bellowing out.
    Inside emblazoned skull,
    dying ember darkness,
    cool and heavy,
    unignited still.
    Or perhaps,
    those final dreams
    also seared and sputtered,
    and too caught afire.

RAPID INVERSE HYPERTRICHOSIS

Eve Harms

"Are you sure you want it?" says Claire. "Jim thinks it killed Bianca."

"I'm pretty sure it was the pain killers and Xanax that killed Bianca," I say and snort a bump of Ketamine off a key. My eyes roll back and I separate from my body, my consciousness lifting two feet above it. A rush of numbness mixed with euphoria surges through me, and for a moment I'm free from this flesh prison; this loathsome parasite that eats away at my vitality, my soul, with every passing second. I savor the weightless moment of no pain, no disgusting physical form, and my gaze floats around Claire's dim living room, watching clear spots dancing over the rutty, off-white walls

Claire waves her hand in front of my face. "Hello, Alli? I said, she was taking the supplement when she overdosed. They never determined the exact cause of death."

I blink, my double vision merges, and my consciousness seeps back into meat. The musty smell of stale air and un-cleaned cat boxes re-enter my nose. The best part of the high is already over. "This is really good K."

"Yeah, it's the human grade stuff. Look, I'll sell you the pills. Just promise you'll be careful with them. Maybe don't take the full dose to start? Just . . . listen to your body, okay?"

I cackle.

Claire takes a bump, and wipes her face with the back of her hand as she snorts, twisting her palm and flexing her fingers. "It's not funny. It's probably fine, but who knows what's in it?"

Branson jumps on my lap and snuggles in with a purr. I stroke his soft fur and scratch his head. "I can't wait any longer to be approved for laser. And it takes years to be permanent anyways. I need this shit off of my face. The pills work, right?"

She smiles and her dark-circled eyes light up. "It's literally incredible. Bianca's face looked hairless within a week."

She pulls out a large pill bottle, the label has no text, just an old photo of Jo-Jo the Dog-Face Boy inside a thick red NO circle. She shakes it with a low rattle that gives away the massive size of the pills and hands it over to me. "It's supposed to be permanent if you finish the bottle. Take five with food everyday until it's gone. And promise you'll be careful."

I study Jo-Jo on the bottle and snort before putting it and my dime baggie of K into my purse. I hand her some cash, and get up to leave. "I promise. And if I die, at least I'll die smooth. Admit it, Bianca never looked better in that casket. Flawless makeup and not even a hint of stubble on her face."

Claire's expression falls. "That's not funny."

She's right. It's not fucking funny at all. I fight the tears welling up in the corner of my eyes. "Yea."

Claire hugs me. "I know."

I grasp her tight, and the tears flow with sobs. "I'm fucking tired of losing people."

"Me too. At least her family buried her as Bianca. And you're right, she looked great—like Bianca. She would have been happy about that."

* * *

I say my goodbyes and head for the breakfast burrito place a couple blocks away. And it's never too late in the day for a breakfast burrito. I'll get a diet soda to wash down these no-hair pills and finally rid myself of this fucking beard shadow. My cis friends say it's not noticeable, but they're just being nice. I see it. On myself and other trans women.

I keep my eyes ahead, and try to avoid the gaze of the two bros about to pass. White tank tops show off their tanned and buff arms that fill me with fear and a touch of horniness. Their heads turn slightly toward me as they walk with a forceful ease and I hope I blend in. They're so strong—I wouldn't stand a chance if they decided the world would be better with one less freak. I can feel their gazes, even through the mirrored sunglasses—clocked. Heads turn to further scrutinize as they pass.

It's all over my face. It doesn't matter how much makeup I put over it. They can see the shadow. Or my broad shoulders or large brow or the numerous other tells. They can smell the M on my birth certificate, and laugh at me to each other when I'm out of earshot. At least they didn't stop.

I'm a freak. A fucking joke. I'm not a real woman. If I looked like those perfect trans women on YouTube—maybe I'd feel different. They're real. Unclockable. I try to shake off the thoughts. I'm real. I'm real. I'm real and a shit-person for thinking otherwise.

I almost miss the burrito place. With a breath I open the door and get in line. I check Twitter to see if my latest tweet got any likes—no, but a stranger replied: *You're a big fat hairy*

97

man masquerading as a woman. You think wearing makeup and dresses is all it means to be a woman? It's worse than blackface.

It's like a punch in the gut—I should stop posting about trans stuff. I want the blow to shrink me until I disappear.

"Sir? It's your turn to order."

My heart sinks and my cheeks flush. What is it about me? Full face of makeup, women's jeans and a low cut blouse, long hair—what else do I need to do to get a ma'am?

I order my burrito and a diet soda. He probably doesn't mean anything by it. I've been coming here forever and he's just used to the old me. Even if I get rid of the shadow, he'll still see it. I should have moved to a different city after coming out.

I want another bump. I could go do it in the bathroom real quick—except they're fucking gendered of course. I'll take a selfie and post it on Instagram instead. Everyone's nice there, a few likes won't hurt. I sit down and position my head just right to snap a photo. It looks okay. I load it into my face editing app, smooth my skin, lighten up the beard shadow as much as I can, make my nose smaller. I type up the caption: *Just getting a breakfast burrito lol, might delete later.* Eating my burrito and sipping my soda, I check the comments: *You're looking great, sister!* I reply with a thank you and hearts, but the warm fuzzy feeling cools with the realization that she's just humoring me. Would she call a cis woman *sister*? She doesn't see me as a woman—she never will.

I crack open the pill bottle and toss five in my mouth, almost choking as I wash them down.

* * *

Day two. I wake up with a splitting headache. Tumbling out of bed, tangled in blankets, I land almost flat on my face. A headache is normal, but this one is bad, really bad. My whole body aches.

I put on my tucking panties and stumble to the fridge—it's empty except for a pallet of sugar-free energy drinks. I crack one open—I love that sound—and down it, letting the piss-colored liquid burn my throat and empty stomach. I wipe off my mouth, squeeze the can half-assed and toss it, missing the recycling to join the rest scattered on the floor. I'll pick them up later. Maybe I shouldn't drink that stuff, another thing that'll kill me. It's basically poison, but that's one of the things I love about them.

In the bathroom, I splash water on my face. My reflection looks like shit. Is that really what I look like? Stubble sprouts out from my cheeks and chin and under my nose. It grows so fucking fast. I crack open another energy drink and take five more pills. It's been less than 24 hours, but I'm sure it'll be fine.

* * *

Day five. I have the biggest grin on my face, and barely any stubble. Just a few dots here and there. My head is pounding, and I squint my eyes as they adjust to the light in my bathroom. I tie my hair back and apply foundation. I don't have to cake it on, and unless you look closely, the shadow is gone—and I feel lighter without it clinging to me. I text Claire:

Me: It's fucking working!

Claire: Yasss! Let's celebrate. Come over, I just got some new flower.

Me: K. I need to finish putting on my makeup and get dressed.

She sends a flurry of eye roll emojis, and: I'll see you in three hours, then.

I send her a STFU gif. An hour, tops.

I put my phone on silent and work on my eyes, not screwing up my eyeliner for once. The pen glides across my lids, and I flick it to create perfect wings on each side. I put on lipstick, shaping my lips, and they turn out perfectly symmetrical. I brush my hair; it's shinier and healthier than ever which is an unexpected but welcome side effect. I sigh with relief, looking myself over in my full-length mirror before I go. I almost look like a cis woman. Almost unclockable. Maybe I could live with this body—with a few surgeries and a few less pounds.

I pop five pills—forty left—before I grab my keys and head out to Claire's.

She's already high. "Wow, on time for once."

"Don't be a buzzkill."

"I'm your dealer. I'm pretty sure that makes me the opposite of a buzzkill."

"Oh, you're my dealer today? Does that mean you're charging for my *celebration*?"

She drags me inside and plops me on the couch. My ass is now covered in cat fur—it's all over the couch. "Is Branson having a shedding problem or something?"

She shoves a pipe with a fresh bowl in my face. "Shut up and smoke, dummy."

Maybe it's a little early to smoke. I still feel like I'm waking up, and this will definitely destroy me for the rest of the day. The weed smells sweet and tangy. It's my day off—and I've earned it. I take the pipe, put it up to my lips, and light up.

Claire inspects my face. "Incredible. It's totally gone. How do you feel? Any side effects?"

Distracted by her question, I take the hit too long and burn my throat. I pull back but not fast enough and cough in Claire's face. She hops back. "Alli! Gross!"

I try to apologize, but I can't stop coughing, my throat burns, my head feels like it's about to burst with every spasm. Claire is in the kitchen, probably cleaning my spit off of her face. My throat is raw, I can't stop coughing, but I manage to croak out "Water. . .water" when she steps back into the room. She disappears with an exasperated cry and reappears with a glass of water and an active bitch face.

I chug the cool water, and it begins to soothe my throat. I swallow a few times and take some more sips until I can speak again. "My headaches are much worse. But other than that, no side effects. I only have eight days left."

"So we have a glowing recommendation then?"

I take a sip of water. My throat still itches, but it doesn't feel like it's because it's raw. It's like there's something stuck in there. I try and clear it out, the sound is loud, and raspy, and deep. "Yea, definitely."

She's saying something else about me being a guinea pig, but I can't concentrate on it. What the hell is in my throat? Cat hair?

I stumble into her cramped bathroom and slam the door behind me. The light is harsh—like a call center or a Walmart—and I'm overwhelmed by the clutter of makeup, shampoo bottles, and skin products. Fuck. I'm really high.

I bend my tongue so the back of it runs up and down the top of my esophagus. There's definitely something back there. I worm my index and middle finger down my sore throat, feeling the back of my tender gullet and holding my gagging back. It's a long piece of hair, maybe two. It's too long to be Branson's, I must have inhaled one of Claire's. The hairs slip in and out of my fingers, too slippery to grasp, until I adjust my fingers so I can pinch with my nails. Got it.

I pull the strands, they're almost out of my mouth, but they catch—and I feel them tugging on my throat. I tug at them again, harder, and I gag as I feel the lining of my esophagus painfully stretching. I remove my fingers and open my mouth wide and look in the mirror, bobbing up and down, trying to catch the light so I can see down my throat and find out what the fuck is in there. My hands are shaking as I take my phone out of my purse, and I take a flash photo down my gullet.

Swallowing, I feel the hairs rustle. I steady myself as the room shifts. I shouldn't have hit the pipe so hard. I turn the phone around to view the photo. There are thin silky brown hairs, some hanging down the back of my throat, some tangled and stuck to the moist lining inside. They're mine, and they're growing inside me!

Screaming, I drop my phone on the floor. The shag carpet of the bathroom lightly tickles my palms and knees as I retrieve it. What the fuck is Claire thinking with a carpeted bathroom? It's disgusting. Has it always been this way—and I never noticed? God, I'm so high.

Doesn't matter, I have to get these fucking hairs out of my throat. Now. Claire's knocking on the door. "You okay in there?"

The esophagus hairs are lengthening, growing, I can feel them inching down my throat ever-so-slightly. "I'm fine! Do you have any scissors?"

"Yeah, in the medicine cabinet. You sure you're okay?"

I push myself off of the floor, breaking the light grip of the shag carpet's tendrils. "Yes! Has your bathroom always had this long carpet?"

"What are you talking about? Alli!"

The scissors are long and heavy, all metal—meant for an office. I open the blades—Jesus they must be at least six inches—the sharp edges are rusty. Is this what she uses to cut her choppy bangs? They close with a sound of scraping metal and a clank. I open my mouth, throw my head back like a sword-swallower, and try to relax my jaw and throat, lowering the blades of the scissors inside, toward the hairs, trying to keep my hands steady. I can feel the pointy tips at the back of my throat, and I lightly probe the sore lining, searching for the small cluster of hairs. One of the hairs moves, pushed by the blade, and it grazes the other side of my esophagus.

My hand jiggles as I open the scissors slightly and snip. Did I get any of them? I can't be sure. Claire bangs on the door, and I almost jump, but I tense all of my muscles up immediately to stop myself. I don't stab myself through my throat, but my tensed-up esophagus squeezes around the blades, stretching and scraping it.

She bangs again. "What are you doing in there?"

I wiggle the scissors around, snipping quickly, hoping to get the hairs. I pull the blades out, four strands caught inside. Thank god, I think that's all of them. I turn to the door. "I'm fine!"

I'm fine.

* * *

Day nine. I roll out of bed. My head feels like it's being squeezed by a giant hand. Like it's going to burst—but I'm used to the headaches. I'm still taking the pills. I tried to stop, but my beard shadow came back, darker and thicker than ever. Clocked, clocked, clocked—shame on my face. Everyone laughing, everyone on the planet. And now, the shadow is almost completely gone. Just four more days of pills, including today, and it'll be gone forever.

Seventeen missed calls and a bunch of texts—probably Claire. I roll my tongue around in my mouth, feeling the silky hairs that grew overnight. I bought a nice, clean pair of scissors to take care of them.

I'm getting used to removing the hair growing in my throat, inside my nostrils, and out of my gums. It's just like shaving my body, and the rest of the daily chores that keep living in it bearable. I just need a good tool to get rid of the hair covering the walls and ceiling. It's getting really long, and it's always rippling. It would be beautiful if it weren't unnerving.

I'll look up gardening tools later.

* * *

The grainy black and white image flickers into view on the screen. My head, in profile, sliced in half. My brain, my tongue, my throat—all visible for inspection. But it's full of strands starting just behind my face, weaving down my throat, slithering into my nasal cavity, tangled around—and worming

104

into—my brain. The doctor, he's telling me—oh god, his beard's so long and snaked all around the floor, the tiles disappear underneath it. I ask him to repeat himself. He says he's never seen anything like this—he can't believe I'm not dead.

My head spins, the room divides into long, swirly streaks. It has to be a mistake, there has to be something wrong with the MRI machine.

There's only two more days left.

DETACHMENT

Andrés Menéndez

I jumped at the small scream of pain Jan let out. She had blood coming out of her finger, covering the tip like she had put it in a bucket of red paint. She took a napkin from her purse and started to clean her finger to look for the cut. She was distracted by her thoughts most of the time, so she probably turned the page too fast and got hurt. I continued to read my book when Alice talked.

"Do you want to go with Nurse Evans? It looks like a lot of blood," she asked, watching as Jan used a second napkin to stop the flow of blood.

The blood wasn't stopping. Jan rose from the chair.

"It was probably a deep cut. I better go to the nurse to get it clean. I will be back in a few minutes," said Jan while giving us a smile. She started to walk to the entrance of the library.

"Should we go with her?" I asked as I watched her walk.

"She will be fine. And now we have some time to tell you that I love you without being embarrassed by our friends," said Alice. She leaned in to give me a kiss.

I let out a small laugh as we separated and continued to work on our project. We had been together for two years, but our friends would still laugh when we kissed or said something romantic. We always laugh because it's funny, but it's better when they are not around to make us uncomfortable.

"I talked to Martha earlier, and she told me the Thompson twins are having a party on the weekend. We could go if you want," said Alice, eyes on her notebook.

"The twins? I don't like them that much," I responded.

"Me neither, but it could—"

Her words were cut by a scream that came from the hallway outside. Alice was fast to run to the entrance, leaving her bag behind, and I followed her, finding Jan laying on the floor.

"What happened? Are you—?"

When I got close enough, I felt my stomach turn and I wanted to throw up, but the fear that invaded my body from looking at the blood coming out of Jan's leg made me freeze.

She tried to stand up, but there was a lot of blood and she kept slipping. It would only take me five steps to get close enough to help, but the idea of touching any blood killed that thought. It was an amount of blood that couldn't have come from her finger alone. I saw exposed flesh and felt tears sliding down my cheeks.

Her left leg was separated from her body, like it had been cut clean through the thigh.

My brain couldn't comprehend what I was seeing. This was impossible. A limb couldn't separate itself from the body without being cut. But somehow her leg had detached.

"Help me," was all she said, looking at us as she started to cry.

I covered my mouth when I realized that what was coming out of her eyes wasn't water. Thick blood slipped slowly down her cheek, and stopped at the chin.

Alice took my hand and pulled me close to her, guiding me slowly back down the hallway.

"We have to go, Sam," said Alice, walking without taking her eyes off our friend.

"But she—"

I couldn't finish the sentence. Jan extended her arm, reaching out her hand. The finger that was bleeding earlier wasn't cut. It was falling off. And it wasn't the only one. The thumb was the only thing left on her hand which wasn't bleeding.

We ran. The horrifying picture of my friend bleeding was already marked in my memory. I took one last look at Jan. Her right eye popped, blood and pus coming out of the hole.

We would have continued to run without direction if I hadn't remembered our other friends. They would be in our classroom, looking for the books they had left before going to the library.

"Stop, we have to find Martha and Jason," I said.

Alice nodded, turning her head just enough for me to see she had heard me.

It took us a few minutes to reach the classroom. We stood in front of the door for what felt like hours until Alice opened it. I entered with her, both glad and afraid to see that we were alone.

"They should have been here," I said.

I couldn't stop the tears. One of my best friends was dead and the other two were missing, or dead too. Why was this happening? Was I going to end up like Jan?

Alice hugged me. That made me feel better. Safe.

"Just breathe. We can think about them once we are safe. You are strong babe, you can do this," she said, kissing me.

She must have been suffering like I was. But she was thinking about us. About *me*. I couldn't let her efforts be for nothing. I would do what I could to help her.

Then the smell hit me. A metallic scent, similar to rotten meat. Alice gagged, then went to the trash can to throw up. I covered my nose, trying to breathe through my mouth. It felt raw.

Looking to the back of the classroom, I found what was causing it. I walked slowly towards the lump, obscured by chairs and tables. A sound came from further back, but I ignored it, moving closer to the thing on the floor. Closer enough to see shades of black, white and pink. Something red too.

The smell was so strong that I had to fight my urge to leave. Just two more steps and I was close enough. The bile came fast before I could find a place to throw up.

It was like meat that had been minced and then mixed again to form a pink dough. The black and white were clothes, left behind once the body had melted. Under the mountain of meat was a pool of blood, steam rising from it.

It must have been Jason. There was no way to prove it but for the thick black glasses next to the t-shirt. We had seen him use them every day since elementary school.

I wanted to scream, but I froze when I saw Martha in the back of the classroom. She made the same sound I'd ignored before, and started to get close. The fine line of sanity was in danger of snapping as I saw how she looked.

She moved with her hands, using her strength to pull herself closer. It was like she had been slashed in half. There was no sign of her lower body. The sound she made wasn't speech.

Her open mouth revealed a few teeth and no tongue. Only blood remained.

Alice's scream made me move. I took her hand and ran to the door, pushing her so she could be the first to get out. Hearing Martha try to speak made me look back at her. She was crying, her eyes describing the confusion and fear she was living.

I walked out and closed the door behind me. The air was heavy as I breathed and I fell to the ground. This must be a nightmare. I must have hit my head and I was dreaming. That's what I wished was the truth. But it wasn't. My friends were dead and only we remained.

We had been together since elementary school, the five of us against the world. So many laughs that we shared, joking about our classmates. All the crying we did when someone was hurt or needed company. The parties we had gone to and how much happiness I felt with them.

All of it came back in a flash to my brain and I couldn't stop crying. They were my friends and I loved them with all my heart, but there was nothing I could have done for them. I needed to survive.

"We need to find help," I said, standing up.

Alice was looking at the door in front of us. Blood was coming from under it. Knocking came from the other side.

"*Alice*. We have to go."

She turned to look at me, and it was the first time in our relationship that I had seen her afraid. What was happening was horrible and it was starting to get to her.

I took her hand moved her away from the classroom. We only walked a little when Alice stopped.

"I can't do this," she said looking into my eyes.

"We can find someone. Its Friday, the basketball team should be practicing in the gymnasium," I said.

The gym was at the end of the hallway. It wouldn't take long to get there. I gave Alice a hug. I could feel that she was deciding if she wanted to give it back.

"I can't do this without you," I said, and she finally hugged me.

We stood there for a few minutes, but it felt like seconds. Being by her side made me feel that everything would be okay. That I wouldn't end up like Martha or Jan or even Jason. We just needed to get to safety. We started to run down the hall.

The entrance to the gymnasium had two big doors that were usually closed unless the basketball team had to practice. As we came closer to them, I saw that one was halfway open. Someone was in there.

I realized we had made a mistake seconds before Alice pushed on the door. The smell hit me and made me want to throw up again. It was the same one that had come from Jason's body. Or what was left of it. But much stronger.

We came through the door and stopped at the scene. I gagged as Alice threw up behind me. The blood under my shoes was thick. The floor was normally light brown, but now only a fourth of it had its original color. The blood covered the rest.

The basketball team had twenty members including the coach, and all of them were in front of us, looking the same as Jason. Small mountains of flesh were scattered on the floor, the remains of their white uniforms tinted red with blood. Some of the mountains were bigger than the others, and I threw up when I saw two pairs of shorts in one of them.

"Don't look at them. Follow me, we will avoid them," I said, cleaning my mouth with my sleeve.

I pulled Alice close. She couldn't stop looking at our friends and classmates. I gave them one final look. How was something like this possible? They were alive an hour ago, and now they were just minced meat and flesh.

"Alice, look at me. We need to continue," I said.

She turned to look at me. Fear and sickness were the feelings that her face transmitted. But she was still breathing. She was alive. And I'd promised to protect her.

We started to walk behind the bleachers to avoid being near those things. I kept my focus on the path in front of me, and on breathing through my mouth to avoid throwing up again. At the end of the small hall we turned left towards the entrance to the locker room.

"Their backpacks should be in there. We can look for a phone," I said.

I put more grip on her hand and started running. Once we were in the locker room she let go and started to breathe heavily. She must have been containing her breath to avoid the smell too.

I came close and hugged her. She started to breathe normally after a few seconds and then I freed her from my grip.

"Just a few more minutes until we can get help," I said. She just nodded while looking at the floor.

We separated and walked to the lockers that were at the end of the hallway. She started to open the ones on the left, so I checked the ones on the right. There was nothing in the first six except a backpack hanging in one of the bottom lockers. I started to search it for a phone, or anything we could use, but it was empty.

"Samantha," came Alice's voice from the other side.

I turned and my heart dropped.

Blood was coming from her leg. It looked like she had cut her thigh horizontally, the line continuing to extend until it connected to the other end. I ran and caught her as she fell to the ground.

"Just breathe babe. You will be fine, we will get help," was all I could say while I pulled her closer to me, her head now resting on my chest.

I felt blood on my right hand. I had rested it on Alice's, which was bleeding too, just like her leg, the cut growing from one side until it surrounded her entire arm. The limb started to separate from her body, more blood dropping on the floor.

"I never told you how much it meant to me that you gave me a Coral Doll on my birthday," she said, moving my face with her remaining hand so I could look at her. She was crying, but the smile she had was of happiness.

"My mother told me that it took you two months to find it. You even had to visit garage sales," she continued.

"You really wanted that doll," was all I could say. My throat hurt with each word, and the tears wouldn't stop.

"When I opened the box at the party and saw it, it felt like the first time we kissed at Allison's birthday. Like it was a defining moment in my life."

At the top of her head, a small drop of blood started to move down her forehead. I tried to clean it with my hand but it kept coming.

"I love you Sam. You are the love of my life," she said. I didn't know if she could feel the line of blood coming down her nose.

"I love you too Alice," I said, trying to smile but failing as I continued to cry.

I remembered the happiest moment I had lived with her. It was our visit to the amusement park. One minute we were riding a roller coaster and the next we were entering a clown show. The amount of food we ate that day was bigger than what I ate alone in an entire week. It felt like we were alone in the universe, existing and living together. There was no homework to bother us, no parents looking at what we did in public. I was happy to feel like life was beautiful because of the moments I would live with Alice.

"Do you think the police will find us here?" she said with a weak voice, taking me out of the journey I was having in my head.

"They will. We just have to wait here," I said, looking at her face now divided in half by the blood that continued down her chest.

"I can wait here as long as you are with me."

"I will not leave you babe."

Would somebody save us? I didn't know how many students and teachers were in the school. And I didn't think they would look for someone in the locker room. But I couldn't tell her that in her last living moments.

We waited.

QUICK, THINK OF A NUMBER BETWEEN NONE AND DEAD

David Sandner

As he tunneled, naked, through the piled dead, they stank, reeking like bile, parching his mouth, stinging his eyes; they creased between his toes; their fluids dripped, streaming down his body. He no longer feared the dead; he only wept for them at unknown intervals, without warning or forethought, and when it was done, he pressed on digging, unthinking; but he hated the smell because he knew it loathed him back: the stink stunned his thoughts and assailed his sanity—he did not know how long he had heaved against the heaps of putrefying bodies, climbing always up; the smell obliterated every coherent idea: even his name and history. He had no identity but darkness and the ever present smell.

No sky hung above him, only the corpses packed so tightly he had to struggle to pull them loose to make his way up. They oozed, excreting an awful rain . . . or as if crying, a steady wash of blood, bile, vomit, urine and decaying flesh.

To burrow past bodies is painstaking work. He would spend uncountable hours in a dark pocket of rank air, a rough six-by-six, lined by bodies, waiting for the energy to press on. He had an instinct for *up* and nothing more. The roof of rotting flesh never fell in, held together by its sticky matter. The floor in the dark below him was thick with the viscous fluids leaking from the dissembling bodies on which he had his being. There was the idea of *light* in his mind, but he could not imagine that light falling on anything distinct, like a loved one's face; there was nothing he longed to see, but he desperately wanted to feel the touch of light on his face. And he would have killed all those piled up bodies dead once again for a cool breeze on the back of his neck. How many hours? How many days had he climbed?

By careful prying, prodding at an arm or torn rib, shaking a cold hand hanging down, or pulling on a shoulder, broken and twisted—by such stratagems he would pry loose a corpse from the ceiling, separating it from the dried muck of blood and body matter that stuck it there. Usually, of course, he would only get parts of a body, an arm or leg or something else unidentifiable; but remarkably, some of the bodies still came more or less whole into his hands. He would set the dead down below his feet, step up on it, and reach to the roof of his cramped and reeking world; then he would poke and shake and pull another body down. Another body and another and another body, for how long he didn't know. He worked on against the limits of death until he grew tired and fell aching into sleep.

The stink colored his dreams. He could close his eyes and imagine some place beyond the piled corpses but the bodies would still litter his thoughts, sitting, hollow-eyed, in straight-backed chairs in the corners of rooms, or face down in fields, or waiting behind every door, or gazing up as his reflection in a clear mountain lake. He would curl in a fetal position, his hands—dried with blood and other matter—clenched to his chest, his head tucked in—and try to shut them out—but the smell! Always! He tasted the metallic tang of blood, but it dulled as the sweet smell of decay never did. So even his dreams were corpse-filled, and he would awake exhausted, their weight endless upon his mind as they were packed in and hanging over his head.

Often gas would escape through mouth, butt cheeks, nose, eye sockets, ruptured ears, and any other new orifice; sometimes they gurgled, bubbled, even squeaked; these sounds—the sighs of the melancholy dead, like unseemly snickers at his plight, or sneers—they haunted him . . . but the sound was never so utter as the smell, terrible and penetrating through everything until there was only the smell. Only the smell.

You must understand it was the smell. He hated it. It hated him. But without it, he certainly would have given up, laid down, expired. The smell moved him, motivated his efforts to escape. The smell was his only friend, his only reason when all other reason had fled. He did not rise toward some significant other, waiting for him. He did not care to live at all. But he could not abide the smell. So he dug and he dug through the dead.

Sometimes he met another tunneler. They met without joy. It didn't matter or change things. Each felt ashamed. They knew that in their tunneling through corpses they desecrated the dead . . . and each knew there was no reason to their desecration, no place to strive toward, and yet they could not stop. Neither believed in some salvation to be found at the end or dreamed of anything but some small relief from the stink. When they came upon one another, they mumbled a guttural surprise and hurriedly felt one another's bodies in the dark. They might have sex. Gender was meaningless. The idea of procreation was absurd in such circumstances. A moment of shared warmth might find them together. An unshareable loneliness and humiliation would leave them tunneling upwards again soon after, but angled away from one another. They did not talk about where they tunneled from any more than they wished to talk about where they tunneled to—it was the same. They did not know. Nameless, furtive, thoughtless, they passed by. They passed on.

What did he eat? What was there to eat? What do we eat that is not the product of the cycle of life and death? He ate quickly without pleasure when his mouth and his stomach demanded. He salted the rot with his tears. Often he ate and fell even deeper into the abyss of sleep, distended with the putrescence he digested. Such sleep piled the corpses ever higher, even in his dreams. He awoke exhausted. He ate as little as he might. He thought as little as he could while he did so.

In odd moments between mindless eternities, he felt engulfed with a strange tenderness. He would handle the corpses gently then, with the vague notion that any could be a parent, a sibling, a lover, unseen in the dark. He would lay the body down and straighten its useless shreds of clothing, pet down its brittle hair, pat its hollowing cheek with love. The moments fell away as mysteriously and quickly as they came. They had no meaning except when he was in them.

When, at last, he tunneled out—after how many hours, years, days, decades, he could not say—what he found did not explain much. He gasped to be able to see at all; his eyes hurt at the sudden twilight above him. Pushing his hand through a hole he made, he saw his skin stained reddish black, wrinkled and old, with a dark rot under his fingernails, held up against an impossible sky beyond. Dizzyingly, the sky lay not above him, but below: clouds swirled over a world set out far *below* him. He realized himself to be on a moon made of the dead, a strange satellite of corpses, circling a dream of the world he had once known.

Dim memories twitched. He had a flash of what it all meant, but he tried to let it go by without leaving a mark. Who could bear it? His vision blurred with tears, yet still he gazed at the sky covering earth and oceans. How many uncountable millions of corpses did it take to aggregate this moon? How beautiful had been the dark world that lay, unreachable now, below him? He had lived there; they all had, once.

He remembered explosions; so many more bodies must have been flung out into empty blackness that did not coalesce into this moon of their failure. Many must have been swept up into it as it spun above the broken earth. It was, of course, impossible. His fragmented memories must be wrong, but he had no others. He cried bloody tears that dried on his face, a face caked with the drippings of decay. The world below him was not his any more; he could see, even now, bits of gray breaking through the black as it sprang to life again. To have refused it, as they all had, as he had, was equally impossible. But they had done it, out of spite. To be still alive, that was impossible. All impossible.

Being dead would have been at least reasonable and sane. But this?

After a tortured time, he turned from the uncertain light and began to burrow, certain he would forget everything again. Or that it would be over at last somehow if he just kept on, just a while longer. He wondered how many times he had done exactly the same thing. And how many times he would do it again.

Then there was nothing but the smell. You must understand it was the smell. It obliterated everything, even memory. How he hated it. He would hate it forever.

CERAMIC SMILE

A. Katherine Black

I escaped that porcelain hell riding in the pocket of my would-be executioner.

It's a miracle she even recognized me. Can't imagine I'd have done what she did, back when I was a person, back when I saw familiar shapes, strangely human images in the grain of some wood or the print of a scarf. If only I'd known, maybe I would've said hello? No, I was a jerk back then. Smug. If I'd seen a face screaming at me from inside a ceramic tile, I'd have congratulated my imagination. Nothing more. Self-absorbed as I was, I would never have stopped to consider the unimaginable truth.

That it might be real.

That was the old me, of course, before I was trapped in the floor of a mall bathroom, unable to blink against the flow of shoes trampling my face. I mean, life in a bathroom floor isn't all bad. Except for the cleats.

I'd say I've adjusted well to my situation, all things considered. It's easiest to handle when the lights are on. It's the darkness, when the pitch black settles over us, that's when things get rough.

It's nothingness. Nothing to see. Nothing to feel. No vibrations, save the occasional wonderful patter of a bug or a rat, but we didn't get those very often. Janitor kept the place clean as a whistle.

Under the merciful florescent glow of mall operating hours, though, I loved watching people come and go. Passing from door to stall, from stall to sink in our humble little bathroom. Sometimes I'd even catch someone glancing my way. They'd pause, head tilted, eyes squinted, and look right at me. Believe me, I absolutely would've said hello, if only I'd known how.

I'd have asked about the weather, even if I could usually tell by their footwear, and wished them a wonderful day, hoping I'd made a tiny difference for a tiny moment in one tiny life on this planet. But I couldn't do that. Because tiles don't have mouths. Or vocal cords. Or breath.

No way I would've been so pleasant back when I actually had a voice.

Memories of life in flesh and motion wilted in that mall bathroom, thinned until they nearly slipped from my disembodied grasp. I do recall, or at least I heavily suspect, that I was very good at slinging insults back then. Distant as that vile version of me had become, still a slant shard of anger remained within my ceramic guts. Enough to recognize the rage stuck in the square prison next to mine.

I didn't see, just as I never saw, how or when Janitor put that someone into that ceramic square near me. He puttered and muttered around the bathroom for long stretches, buffing the floor to a shine until not even a few interesting specks of dirt remained for me to admire and contemplate, and doing who-knows-what else.

There I was, watching the rush of shoes go this way and that, meditating over the lovely designs painted across my face by slushy soles (designs on the bottom of basketball shoes are especially divine) until the bathroom gradually cleared, to my disappointment. And there was only one person left.

Her heels rang a lovely echo as she made her way to the sink. Stepping back to grab a towel, she looked my way, head in that familiar tilt. I pressed against the grout line with every ounce of my weight, as she leaned in. It was more attention than I'd had in, well, how the hell do I know how long? No clock in the bathroom. And then her face fell.

Not fell. *Twisted.*

Faces are fuzzy when people stand, towering at so far a distance, but she bent down. Came into clear focus. Lines formed between her brows. Lips pushed together, like she was trying to solve a puzzle. All at once, her features relaxed and her eyes ballooned to near the size of the lightbulbs above the mirrors. I felt the tremor of her feet shaking in her shoes.

She wasn't looking at me. Thank Janitor for that. It was the tile next to me.

She fell to the floor with a gasp. Her rear slammed onto what might have been other souls in other ceramic squares. (Only Janitor knew how many there were.) And then she scampered up and out the door.

My adrenaline would've been pumping after that scene, if I'd still had glands, organs and blood and such. But of course I don't, and yet I still felt it. Because I'd been seen. Not just seen, recognized. Well, almost recognized. Someone like me was recognized, which meant we all were. Elation, excitement, and joy all crammed into my tile self.

I didn't realize it then, but that was the beginning of the end for our mall bathroom.

It was wintertime, or so the shoes told. Seasons are so easily read on a shoe, toes covered or not, soles mud-smeared or not, and I so loved the winter. Sports teams withdrew with their cleats in hibernation, slush slopped around the floor in the loveliest patterns. Soles slapped wet earth across my face in fascinating designs that slowly shifted dark to light as the moisture escaped, causing the dirt to crack in the most interesting ways. Life as a bathroom tile passes mercifully quickly when there's something to see. That is until Janitor comes to sweep the patterns away and turn off the lights.

I suspect I said something awful, maybe did something awful to him back then, whenever then was, when I was a person. Awful enough to warrant an eternity fused into the floor of a mall bathroom. Did I make a mess? Make a face? Maybe I didn't do anything, ignored him. There are so many ways to hurt someone.

I think it may have been coffee that sent my soul on this wayward path. My memories reek of roasted beans and foamed milk. Of anger at my lovely addiction spilled across the mall floor. I might've let loose some vile insult while I watched Janitor clean my mess. Maybe horrible words were spoken, or maybe they just swam around my brain, yet somehow Janitor still heard. How could he have heard my thoughts? Well, how in the name of Clorox and Lysol was he able to trap souls in his bathroom prison? Yeah, I wonder, too.

It was exciting at first, after that woman ran from our bathroom, the way people looked at the new tile. Even from way down here, I could make out their eyes ballooning. Vibrations from all the frantic footsteps tickled at my insides.

More people came, more people recognized us. Or at least one of us.

Until slushy footprints grew less frequent, and I missed even the boring shoes, the pointless dressy ones with no treads at all. People came through the door fewer and farther between. Lights remained off most of the time, leaving us fused to the emptiness, grouted into nothingness.

Until that time Janitor came in and cleaned nothing. Just stared. *Glared.* At every one of us in turn.

I hadn't realized how many we were. He pressed his face against all of us. Tiles, sinks, mirrors, even something in the stalls—toilets?—and the stall walls themselves. I shivered in my grouting as he crept closer. Vertigo isn't something I thought a tile could even feel, but that's exactly what hit, when he finally turned on me.

His eyes probed my every pattern and scratch. I screamed silently, pressed thin under his narrowed eyes. I pulled away as best I could, backed against the bathroom foundation, but it made no difference. There was no escaping the things I saw, in the pattern of his wrinkles, in the scarring across his forehead, in the crescents cut under his eyes. As if a hundred souls were burned into his skin, wailing, begging for an impossible freedom. The bathroom floor hadn't felt like a mercy until then.

"Bad batch, you lot," he said, turning a slow, crooked dance around the bathroom. His voice soaked heavy into the fabric of our surroundings. "Best be done with ya. Misbehavin' villains." And the lights went out. Stayed out for what felt like an age. Stayed out until I started to wonder where I was, what I was. If I was. No more glorious footprints and slushy winters. Sanity slipped, or whatever version of sanity life as a tile in a bathroom mall might allow.

It was all because of that tile next to me. If only I could have reached out and punched it, the one who ruined it for us all. If only it had eyeballs I could scratch right out. If I could have insulted it, cursed it, maimed that tile, I suspect I would have. Its hatred had been a tsunami, scooping us all up, carrying us all toward destruction. I would have made it feel my own. I pulled against the grout until my surface bulged in the depths of darkness. Selfish tile. Stupid, monstrous tile.

After an eternity, the lights flicked on, bathing our room in a merciful glow. Spilling color and warmth across the faces of all of us trapped souls. A peacefulness soaked in, as boot soles moved across the floor once again, showing us their thick, captivating patterns.

And then they began. Tearing our world apart.

Raw and awake in my grout, without eyelids, without a brain requiring sleep, I witnessed every minute of the destruction. Hammers crippled stalls before they were torn from their roots and thrown to land with a horrific metallic screech. Toilets and sinks, by then coated in the dust of abandonment, were cracked and ripped away in gruesome fashion.

All the screams. All those souls, ripped from their mall bathroom world.

The floor was last.

Jackhammer. The word from my former life slammed into my thoughts when I saw the machine carried into our bathroom. Its motor kicked into life, and in a far corner, it began smashing my kind. Its roar was savage, like Janitor's laughter when he'd walked out the door that very last time. The machine moved in my direction. Its howl slipped distant as my thoughts swirled, slowed.

What happened to a broken tile? Would its soul crack and split, torn into jagged fragments? Would it be freed, or would it be forever splintered, crying out for its missing parts?

Shards of shattered tile flew into the air as the jackhammer moved closer. Only a few tiles away now. What's the fate of a tile, once smashed beyond repair? Soon I would know. I would know thanks to the newcomer soul, the one who ruined everything with its unchecked malice.

What would I do with my fury? Did I really think I could unravel hate's result by spewing more of the same? And how would I do that? I had no idea how that tile was able to communicate with all those people, how it passed its hateful image on to others. And if I could, why would I want to be anything like that sorry piece of ceramic?

Grout fractured against my square as the hammer approached. Its motor shook the very walls, permeated my insides, told me this was it. This life or whatever it was, this existence I'd been granted as a result of my own rage, would be over in minutes thanks to the hateful acts of another. Would I leave this life in the same sorry state I left the last one?

The jackhammer's steel end slammed up and down with terrifying speed, pulverizing everything it touched. As my neighbors were snapped and ground to bits, the machine's tremendous vibrations shook my own soul into a strange rhythm. A rhythm woven with an unexpected thread of calm.

How would I meet my end? How about this—

Pressing my tile face upward, I pushed myself out as far as I could, straining to meet my executioner with all the joy I could summon. Damn the hatred. To hell with anger. I called to mind all the exquisite mud prints from so many shoes that passed across my surface, the smiles and laughter exchanged between bathroom visitors, children and parents, co-workers and best-friends. I even recalled sights former-me used to notice, breathtaking sunsets, birds fluttering through trees, fresh steps through newly fallen snow, and I smiled. I smiled the warmest, happiest, most delightful smile I could imagine, pushing that smile up and out until the grout cracked on every side.

The hammer stopped.

A resounding silence met with the new tranquillity within my tile, as the hammer was laid against so many broken souls strewn across the bathroom floor. Its wielder bent her knees and peered into my face. Warm breath caressed my surface. Lines of amusement formed around her mouth and eyes.

She stood and retrieved her hammer.

Serenity remained within my ceramic self, even as the jackhammer roared back to life. At least I'd made someone happy. It was good, as parting gifts go. The floor jolted and ripped around me. Even if I'd had eyelids, I would not have closed them. Destruction danced heavy, crushing the last of the tiles. Slivers of other damned souls flew across my view. Yet the hammer did not touch me.

In what would have been only a few heartbeats, if I'd had a heart, it was done. People came with shovels to remove the carnage, while the one who should've been my executioner bent down and tapped at my sides, showering me with gentle shivers, until I was free. A soft breeze brushed at my underside as she picked me up.

Cradled in her hand, I flew above the destruction in the mall bathroom. My view shifted from the ruination below to the face of my rescuer, who smiled before sliding me into her pocket.

That's when I left my personal hell.

I sit on a shelf above her desk now, in a perfect spot. I can see out the window, watch leaves swirl in the winds and birds congregate around feeders. Every evening my rescuer sits at her desk and watches a glowing screen to my left. Rhythmic keyboard tapping sends wave after wave of soothing vibrations through the desk.

She looks, right at me, at least a few times every night. Feels like I'm floating. Every time I meet her gaze I remember the cushion of her pocket, the warmth of her first smile. And so I try my best to give something back.

I offer pictures, images, splashed across my face. Birds soaring above oceans, towers covered in flowing vine, animals grazing on a mountainside. Of places I nearly remember. Of places I imagine she'd love.

The remainder of my time is spent gazing at clouds through the window, as they shift and twist in grays and blues, forming shapes that remind me one moment of a train, another moment of a lion, yet another of a butterfly. I watch the clouds decorate the sky, and I dream of ways I might say hello.

Author Biographies

A. Katherine Black is an audiologist and a writer. She adores multi-colored pens, stories featuring giant spiders, and nearly anything at 2 a.m. She lives in a small town with her family, their cats, and her overworked coffee machines. Find her at flywithpigs.com or on Twitter @akatherineblack

Die Booth likes wild beaches and exploring dark places. When not writing, he DJs at Chester's best (and only) goth club. You can read his stories in places like LampLight Magazine, The Fiction Desk, Flame Tree Press and The Cheshire Prize for Literature anthologies. His books *My Glass is Runn*, *365 Lies* (profits go to the MNDA), *Spirit Houses* and *Making Friends (and other fictions)* are available online. He's currently working on a collection of spooky stories featuring transgender protagonists. You can find out more about his writing at diebooth.wordpress.com or say hi on Twitter @diebooth

Lorenzo Crescentini was born in Forlì, and currently resides in Rome (Italy). His stories have been published in a number of collections and magazines including Clarkesworld, Weirdbook, ARTPOST magazine, Future Visions, Dream of Shadows among others.

Maxx Fidalgo is a 25 year old queer Luzo-American from the south coast of Massachusetts. He loves writing cosmic and occult horror stories, as well as queer romance. When he's not writing or at his day job, he likes to travel, play his guitar, and sing.

Maija Haavisto has had two poetry collections published in Finland: *Raskas vesi* (Aviador 2018) and *Hopeatee* (Oppian 2020). In English her poetry has appeared or is forthcoming in Wondrous Real, ShabdAaweg Review, The North, ANMLY, Asylum, Eye to the Telescope, Shoreline of Infinity and Kaleidoscope. Find her on Twitter @DiamonDie

Eve Harms is a writer of freaky fun horror fiction and zine maker. Her work has appeared in publications such as Vastarien Literary Journal (under Rayna Waxhead), Creepy Catalog (under Kendra Temples), and her story *The Glow at Home* was featured on Ellen Datlow's recommended list in the anthology Best Horror of the Year Vol. 11. She currently resides in Los Angeles with her children's book illustrator spouse and two cats. You can find her on the web at eveharms.com and on Twitter/Instagram @eveharmswrites

Pedro Iniguez is a speculative fiction writer who also enjoys painting. His work can be found in publications such as Space and Time Magazine, Crossed Genres, and Tiny Nightmares. Originally from Los Angeles, he now resides in Sioux Falls, South Dakota. He can be found online at Pedroiniguezauthor.com.

Ai Jiang is a Chinese-Canadian writer, an immigrant from Fujian, and an active member of HWA. Her work has appeared or is forthcoming in F&SF, The Dark, PseudoPod, Prairie Fire, Jellyfish Review, among others. Find her on Twitter @AiJiang_ and online at aijiang.ca[1]

Joe Koch writes literary horror and surrealist trash. Joe is a Shirley Jackson Award finalist and the author of *The Wingspan of Severed Hands*, *The Couvade*, and the forthcoming collection

---

1.   http://aijiang.ca/

Convulsive from Apocalypse Party Press. Their short fiction appears in Year's Best Hardcore Horror, *Not All Monsters*, Liminal Spaces, and many others. Find Joe online at horrorsong.blog and on Twitter @horrorsong

Basile Lebret is a French blogger. He once was a gaffer on movie sets but decided to better his craft writing stories. He lives South of Paris, in Essonne, where the urban network finally meets the trees, just like Serge Lehman. Follow him on Twitter @BasileLebret or find him online at basile-lebret.medium.com

Sam Lesek is a writer of dark speculative fiction and poetry from Toronto, Canada. Her writing has been published by Scare Street, Ghost Orchid Press, and Black Hare Press. Find her on Twitter @SamLesek.

Avra Margariti is a queer author, Greek sea monster, and Pushcart-nominated poet with a fondness for the dark and the darling. Avra's work haunts publications such as Vastarien, Asimov's, Liminality, Arsenika, The Future Fire, Space and Time, Eye to the Telescope, and Glittership. *The Saint of Witches*, Avra's debut collection of horror poetry, is forthcoming from Weasel Press. You can find Avra on Twitter @avramargariti

Andrés Menéndez (He/Him) lives in Yucatán, México. He likes to use his free time to write about LGBT+ characters in different genres. When he is not writing, he can be found drinking chocolate and reading. You can find him on Twitter @MenendezCAndres

Tiffany Morris is a Mi'kmaw/settler writer of speculative fiction and poetry from Kjipuktuk (Halifax), Nova Scotia. Her work has previously appeared in Nightmare, Uncanny, and

Apex Magazine, among others. Find her online at tiffmorris.com or on Twitter @tiffmorris

H.V. Patterson lives in Oklahoma and is obsessed with all things horror. She recently placed second in the Rural Oklahoma Museum of Poetry's Dark and Scary Poem Contest. She has been published by Not Deer Magazine and Trembling with Fear (Horror Tree). She's a fiction reader for Nimrod International Journal and co-founder of Dreadfulesque (dreadfulesque.com). Follow her on Twitter and Goodreads @ScaryShelley

Sarah Peploe's short stories have appeared in various anthologies including Snowbooks' *Game Over,* Martian Migraine's *CHTHONIC,* and Cursed Morsels' upcoming *Antifa Splatterpunk.* She also writes and draws comics as part of Mindstain Comics co-operative. She lives in York and tweets @SarahPeploe

Stephanie Rabig is a permanently-exhausted cryptid who comes out on the full moon to tell horrible dad jokes. She can be found on Twitter @stephrabig

David Sandner is a member of SFWA and the HWA. His recent novelette, *Mingus Fingers* (Fairwood), co-written with Jacob Weisman of Tachyon Publications, is a fantasy about Jazz and magic that got strongly positive reviews from F&SF ("one of those rare stories that got everything right") and Locus Online ("a wonderful accomplishment"). He has stories/poems in Asimov's, Weird Tales, PodCastle, Realms of Fantasy and many other magazines, and anthologies including The HWA Poetry Showcase, Mike Ashley's Mammoth Book of Sorcerers, Ellen Datlow's *Tails of Wonder and Imagination*, W.P. Kinsella's *Baseball Fantastic,* and so on. His site is davidsandner.com

Lorraine Schein is a New York writer. Her work has appeared in VICE Terraform, Strange Horizons, Enchanted Conversation and Mermaids Monthly, and in the anthology *Tragedy Queens: Stories Inspired by Lana del Rey & Sylvia Plath. The Futurist's Mistress*, her poetry book, is available from Mayapple Press – mayapplepress.com

Angela Sylvaine is a self-proclaimed cheerful goth who still believes in monsters. Her debut novella, *Chopping Spree*, an homage to 1980s slashers and mall culture, is available now. Her short fiction has appeared in multiple publications and anthologies, including *Places We Fear to Tread* and *Not All Monsters*. You can find her online at angelasylvaine.com

Tabatha Wood is an Australian Shadows award-winning author of dark, speculative fiction and emotional, narrative poetry living in Aotearoa, New Zealand. She likes strong coffee, cats and spending time by the sea.

TRIGGER WARNINGS

The following list isn't exhaustive, but it takes into account certain themes and situations included in *Monstroddities:*

- Body dysmorphia
- Cannibalism
- Death of a child
- Depression
- Drug use
- Gore
- Homophobia
- Loss of a child
- Loss of a parent
- Transphobia